STARTING OUT

. . . The world all about her was very large and strange, and she was lost among so many new smells. She was just beginning to feel anxious when a boy who appeared in the doorway leaned down to touch her.

"Hello! Where did you come from? Aren't you pretty!"

The puppy flattened and pricked her ears, unused to the sound of a human voice but liking its tone. Then she found herself being swung into the air, held tight round the middle by two firm hands. Her nose was suddenly close to the boy's nose, a tiny little face beside the human one. Undaunted, the puppy reached out with her tongue and licked the friendly nose.

Helen Griffiths

Just a Dog

Illustrated by Victor Ambrus

AN ARCHWAY PAPERBACK
POCKET BOOKS • NEW YORK

POCKET BOOKS, a Simon & Schuster division of
GULF & WESTERN CORPORATION
1230 Avenue of the Americas, New York, N.Y. 10020

Copyright © 1974 by Helen Griffiths
Illustrations copyright © 1974 by Hutchinson Junior Books

Published by arrangement with Holiday House, Inc.
Library of Congress Catalog Card Number: 74-19025

ISBN: 0-671-56036-0

First Pocket Books printing October, 1976

10 9 8 7 6 5

Trademarks registered in the United States and other countries.

Printed in the U.S.A.

For Carlos and Angelines
Who have twice saved Shadow's life

Contents

1	Hiding Place	1
2	Four Puppies	13
3	Boys	27
4	Two Little Dogs	41
5	A Home of Sorts	55
6	"Get Rid of Her"	67
7	Abandoned	83
8	Winter	97
9	By the Railway	107
10	Nando	119
11	Summer	133
12	A New Friend	147
13	Canela	161
14	A Change of Luck	171
15	The Law Is the Law	183
16	Welcome Home	197
	Epilogue	209

Just a Dog

1

Hiding Place

1

Toward the East the faintest light was beginning to glimmer through the cloudy darkness. It wasn't enough to be called dawn. It didn't spread light to those shadowy parts of the city's outer limits where bright lighting gave way to the solitary bulb, trembling in the breeze on the end of a cable which hung from a wall bracket of a corner house. The shadows were deeper still beyond that dull circle of light but the dog that padded along the dusty lanes needed no light to guide her.

She knew every stone, every rut, every lump of tumbled masonry and, as she was hurrying slightly, she didn't stop to make sure of the scents because she knew them all already. She obviously had some destination in mind as she traversed the length of one lane, cut across another, scurried across a stretch of open ground abandoned to a clutter of rusty tins and rotting refuse, and turned left at the solitary cottage where bread was sold.

Beyond this shabbily whitewashed, red-gabled house, a grapevine clustering its walls and windows, there was only a field; open country that went on and on to the horizon, and the dog had no knowledge of what was beyond because she never troubled herself with futile wanderings.

Now, she only went as far as the line of tumbled-down dwelling places whose bricks and doorposts were strewn at varying distances from their original positions. There was still a roof over one of the rooms, though doors and windows had long been torn out or rotted away. She cautiously scrambled over the sharp-edged bricks and broken glass, for the first time intent upon discovering the meaning of every scent and sound.

The light in the East was slowly extending and there was a definite brightness behind the jumbled colors of receding night. It wasn't sufficient to light up the interior of the ruined cottage. On a clear night the stars reflected light through the holes in the roof but the morning gloaming hadn't their brilliance so the dog had to rely on her ears and nose alone.

At last she was satisfied that everything was as it should be. The only smell was of the damp lime on the crumbling walls and the rusting iron of the kitchen stove. She went forward again, ears pricked, nose sharp, paws treading carefully into the unknown. The breeze that had been ruffling under her hair all this while could not enter and she was suddenly warmer.

She sniffed about the floor which was scattered with dirt and rubbish left by old occupants or dumped by strangers. She knew what she was looking for and wouldn't be satisfied with less. There was a small space between two walls, from one of which dragged a door on broken hinges. The space had once been a cupboard and there was still a shelf above the dog's head.

She tried the space for size, getting down and turning around and around. It was a bit tight—she was a large dog—and the floor was littered with brick dust and chunks of plaster. She scratched about sharply with her claws, snuffled in every corner, sneezing at the accumulation of dust and lime that filled her nostrils, and again tried it out for size and comfort.

Still only half satisfied, she went off to another part of the tiny room to see if she could find something better but the other crannies were damp or drafty or smaller still, and eventually she came back to the cupboard. She prodded at the walls with her strong, brindled muzzle, and then she curled herself around another half dozen times before managing to settle herself to her satisfaction. All her movements were slow, unhurried, deliberate.

Every now and again her big jaws opened as she panted slightly, closing her eyes and opening them again, half dozing. She was a good-looking animal in spite of her rough appearance, with a deal of wolf dog in her, which accounted for the big triangular ears and long muzzle. Her eyes were deep set and there was no wildness in them, in spite of having always lived a homeless vagabond.

She had never had a master. She had never heard one kind word addressed to her. She answered to no name and to no human command and yet there was a gentleness in her demeanor, a natural docility that was wholly doglike. Although she was a scavenger, living as does the fox, the wolf, the jackal or hyena in other places, she was chained to her inherent domesticity, an animal that belonged to man although no man had ever claimed her.

The walls of the houses were her only haven. In the summertime she lay in their shadow to escape the unbearable heat and she had long ago discovered that, in wintertime, the sun's rays striking on the white walls gave out a warmth which couldn't be found elsewhere. When boys threw stones at her she moved away and when they had gone she came back.

Walls were her only refuge, outer walls because she had never known the inside of a house or stable. For this reason she had come now to the abandoned cottages, seeking a safe birthplace for the life stirring so urgently within her. She hadn't come because the old cottage was reminiscent of people and the master she had never had. The smell of humans would have frightened her away directly! She came as the first wild dogs must have come to man's primitive dwellings, needful of the shelters they erected.

So, in the cupboard of the forgotten cottage, four little whelps made their first whimperings, nuzzling blindly into the only warmth and comfort that would ever be theirs by right, and the mother dog watched over them with a gentle expression while the sun broke up the darkness of the sky.

2

In the days that followed the mother dog hardly left her younglings. She was constantly afraid for their safety, although there was no apparent danger in that isolated place, and was immediately alert at the slightest whimper or movement on their part. If she felt hunger she ignored it. Hunger was her usual state so that in her greater anxiety its pangs hardly bothered her.

From time to time she rose to stretch her limbs, causing the pups to complain with snorty whimperings as she dislodged them, but she was soon curled about them again, glad to have them nuzzle into her flank, tucking them well in with her muzzle.

This was not her first litter. She had had enough pups in the past to know exactly how to treat them but this didn't stop her being constantly anxious about them. She licked their ears and eyes, their bellies and bottoms. She kept them cleaner than they would ever be at any future period in their lives. They were all warmth and softness, smelling of milk and satisfaction in their almost semiconscious existence close to their mother's dugs. The only thing that stirred them was hunger, when they began to clamor and scramble with intent activity, digging their paws into their mother's belly, thrusting a blundering littermate aside, heedless of anything but their own particular need.

The mother dog endured their frequent attacks upon her until they sucked her dry. Even then they would have gone on clinging to her had she not dislodged them by standing up and giving herself a good shake. The most persistent would then fall off and, with cocked ears, she would watch to make sure they were all well tucked into each other, giving them a push with her nose if she wasn't satisfied.

When she did at last make up her mind to leave them on their own for a few hours it was because she was absolutely certain that no danger could befall them. In the several days since their birth no living thing had passed that way, not even a bird or a rat. She knew her hiding place was a safe one and at last her fervent anxiety was appeased.

She trotted off unhurriedly, stopping only to glance about in the ruined doorway, and was gone for a couple of hours, filling her empty stomach with whatever rubbish she could find, drinking her fill of the slightly soapy water splashed about the tap where the women rinsed their washing, and finding on her return what she expected to find, four puppies fast asleep, sucking at each other in their slumber and waking with eager whimpers at her approach.

After that she left them daily for an hour or so and the pups didn't miss her. Even when their eyes first opened their vision was so limited, and their knowledge of the world even less, that they hadn't the remotest desire to discover the meaning of the blurry shapes they could now see.

True, they no longer stayed bunched together quite so much. Now and again they made seal-like movements of curiosity in the first stirrings of the urge to use their short, fat legs, but their clumsy struggles took them hardly any distance from each other and certainly not beyond the cupboard. They were still quite helpless and their helplessness at this stage kept them safe.

They grew rapidly, however, especially when their eyes had opened. They had seemed all paws and hungry mouths, their weak blue eyes half buried in the many furrows of their skulls, but soon the tails were long enough for wagging, the legs were strong enough for gamboling upon, and the black button noses were quiveringly eager to dirty themselves in the cobwebs and dust surrounding their refuge.

They spilled out of the cupboard; they chewed indiscriminately at wood splinters, dirty rags and each other; they pounced on each other with surprising ferocity and gurgling growls, and forgot all their wonderful adventures and discoveries just as soon as the mother dog appeared, smelling of warmth and certain joy.

Sometimes the mother dog would play with them but mostly she just tolerated their untiring attacks upon her, taking advantage of their preoccupation with her paws to lick out their ears, very much like a human mother who takes advantage of her child's desire to tell her something by washing his face while he's speaking.

There was no longer room in the cupboard for them all and, as the days were reasonably warm, they slept less and less in the first refuge. The mother dog came less and less frequently to care for them, often returning only when the day was dying, having left them early in the morning. She had less and less milk for them as their demands upon her grew constantly greater and now when they sucked on her there was more pain than pleasure.

They were startled but undismayed when she snapped at them, driving them away from her

empty dugs, not understanding the meaning of this first lesson of unsatisfied appetite. Till now she had been the fount of all their pleasure and the first denial on her part was not to be heeded.

They bothered her again and again, getting themselves knocked over by her sharp movements, intent in their blundering way to get what they wanted, until in desperation she ran away from them because she could not make them learn that she had nothing more to give them when her dugs were empty. The pups were desperate, too, which was why they ignored her angry snappings and efforts to avoid them. They followed her like a ravening horde, having no pity for her feelings, aware only of their own.

The puppies had strong little teeth by this

time. They were forever sharpening them on bits of bricks and wood and stone. They tried to satisfy their ravening appetites with wood splinters and strands of material chewed from the rags in their surroundings and the only time they slept with any satisfaction was when the mother dog came at nighttime with the small offering of milk that still remained.

By this time she was gaunt, hardly more than skull and ribs, legs and tail, but her instinct to survive was as strong as ever. For the moment she continued to return to her younglings night after night because she still had something to give them after a daytime of scrounging. There would come a time when maternal instinct would no longer make demands upon her, when she wouldn't return to her offspring, when they would have to learn for themselves what life was about.

They were already tiring of waiting for her nightly visits and had explored their surroundings from seam to seam, scrabbling under fallen beams, sticking their heads into the old oven, getting frights when things collapsed under them or over them but coming to no harm. Their mother always slipped away while they were sleeping, to ensure that they didn't follow her, but their sense of smell was growing stronger and they could follow her traces for some of the way.

They were somewhat intimidated by the open plain, which seemed so vast to their small eyes and limited vision. The very thorns were as tall as they were and a crack in the dry ground was enough to make them stop and ponder it for quite some time. It was the time of year when the ants were stirring from their winter slumber and there were freshly turned mounds of earth everywhere, with columns of busy creatures marching to and fro, carrying seed husks, dead insects, one tiny grain of soil, each minute creature contributing to the immense society to which it belonged.

The puppies stuck their noses right into the ants' affairs, causing a havoc of scurryings and disorganization. Ants ran over their paws and in and out of their nostrils and the pups snorted and shook their heads with surprise.

One of them found an old, curled-up shoe and they played with it for some time, taking turns to chew at it and perhaps finding something to take the edge off their hunger, for the treasure was laboriously carried home. There wasn't much else to be found on the plain and hunger eventually led them closer and closer to the houses that were inhabited, drawn there by the different sounds and smells.

Too young to have learned anything but the most elemental caution, too hungry to care anyway about anything but satisfying their ravening stomachs, the four gangling youngsters made their first approach to the world of humans, completely unaware of what fate might hold in store for them.

2

Four Puppies

1

The line of cottages on the outskirts of the city formed almost a village of itself. At one time it probably had been a village but the continual and rapid growth of the city which, not long ago, had been far off, had brought it almost to the doorsteps. Blocks of red-brick flats towered above the roofs of the tiny dwellings, some of which were hardly more than holes dug out of the ground, and it was supposed that one day a bulldozer would come to crush into rubble within only a few hours the places where children had laughed and cried and old people had sat in the sun for years and years.

There was a bread shop and a dairy and a grocery store so dark that you could hardly see the names of the tins on the shelves. There were gardens about six feet square, laid with a conglomeration of patterned floor tiles which had been picked up from the rubbish left by the flat builders. In the late afternoons women sat under a few trees with mending in a basket on their laps and toddlers at their feet, to discuss the latest news and scandals. Radios blared, cocks crowed, children screeched, and a suffocating smell rose from the gutters that ran down the center of the lanes, a primitive form of sanitation.

The women threw their rubbish a short distance away from the houses. Chickens, turkeys and ducks would come to peck at it, flapping their wings to frighten off an equally hungry donkey, retreating themselves at the sight of a dog. Cats came more cautiously, when there was no one about, slinking with jungle stealth, wild, indomitable, racing off to some secret place with their prize. Dogs came at any time, gulping down everything indiscriminately, sticking their muzzles into sardine tins, licking the last grain of rice from a clamshell, even chewing up paper if its taste appealed to them.

Children also came to the rubbish dump. They had very few toys, which they were seldom allowed to play with, and they would scrape about in the muck in search of something of interest, tin cans for throwing stones at, bottle caps in place of marbles, rubber shoe heels and any bit of broken plastic which by its shape or color might draw their attention.

When it rained there was mud and great puddles everywhere, while in the summertime the ground was cracked and sandy. There were a few trees near the public fountain and about these were several rows of washing lines, always laden with sparkling, much-mended sheets, shabby overalls and diapers.

The four questing puppies came of a sudden upon this oasis. They were frolicking and joyful for the sun was warm and the smell of everything promising. A couple of women in dressing gowns and slippers took no notice of them, not even when one of the puppies started to lope after them, instinctively attracted. She followed them to the entrance of one of the cottages and then sat back on her haunches, nonplussed, when they disappeared.

After a while she decided to go back to her littermates but then she couldn't remember the way she had come. The world all about her was very large and strange and she was lost among so many new smells. She was just beginning to feel anxious when another human appeared in a doorway, a boy this time, who leaned down to touch her.

"Hello! Where did you come from? Aren't you pretty!"

The puppy flattened and pricked her ears, unused to the sound of a human voice but liking its tone. Then she found herself being swung into the air, held tight around the middle by two firm hands. Her nose was suddenly close to the boy's nose, a tiny little face beside the human one. Undaunted, the puppy's tongue reached out and licked the friendly nose. The boy laughed, making the puppy flatten her ears again.

She wasn't sure whether all these new things happening to her were good or not but when the boy cradled her in his arms, close against his chest, she felt warm and comfortable, just as if she were against her mother's flank. Instinctively she dug her small, hard muzzle into the boy's chest, looking for somewhere to suck. The boy laughed again, delighted by this apparent show of affection, and he called, "Mama, Mama! Look what I've found," running back into the cottage to show off his prize.

The mother, who was one of the women the puppy had followed from the fountain, wasn't impressed. "Hmm!" she exclaimed. "I don't know why you want to pick up a strange dog. He's probably got something wrong with him. Throw him outside."

"But Mama. . . ."

"Do what I say, Manolo. The last thing we want is a dirty animal about the place."

Reluctantly the boy took the puppy outside again and put her down. He turned her over onto her back and tickled the silky white belly with warm fingers, making the little animal squirm with delight. Manolo smiled and went on playing with her, marveling at the tiny, perfect ears, the dark blue eyes, the stiff little tail. He thought he had never seen anything as pretty as this before.

Meanwhile the other three puppies had kept together, following each other from discovery to discovery, fighting over the remains of a rotting fish head of which the ants had already taken command; playing tug-of-war with a broken shopping bag; growling and yelping and forgetting that they were hungry. One of them chased after a chicken which suddenly appeared in front of them and the rest followed suit, yelping high, sharp tones. The chicken disappeared between the legs of a group of boys and the puppies blundered into them, hardly even trying to escape the outstretched hands that grabbed them up, although their little hearts pumped fearfully.

"What shall we do with them?" cried one.

"Where've they come from?" wondered another.

"Perhaps they belong to someone. Let's find out."

Pleased to have any excuse for not giving up their find, the boys wandered along the various lanes, asking whoever they met if they knew who the puppies belonged to. Every now and then they stopped to fondle and examine them, putting them down, picking them up again, and the bewildered animals hardly knew whether to be frightened or comforted by so much attention.

"They don't belong to anyone," one of the boys said at last.

"What shall we do with them?"

"My mother won't let me have a dog. I've asked her before," was one reluctant reply. "She says you can get all sorts of diseases from dogs."

"One of my aunts died from keeping a dog," agreed another.

"Go on with you! How can you die from keeping a dog?"

"She got lumps inside her and the doctor said she'd caught them from the dog."

"Did the dog die too?"

"I don't know. But I know my aunt did."

The boys put the puppies down and formed a circle around them, seven pairs of eyes watching them with doubt, curiosity and regret. The puppies huddled together, pleased to be left alone at last. One licked its nose, another started to scratch its ear and fell over in the attempt, and the third was animated by this into pouncing on the second's waving tail.

"I'm going to take one home," decided the eldest boy at last. "I bet my father says I can keep it. I don't believe you can catch diseases from dogs, otherwise no one would have them. And lots of people have got dogs, haven't they?"

His companions nodded but the one with the deceased aunt said warningly, "Well, don't say I didn't tell you."

"Which one are you going to have?" was the next question and all seven gave their opinions.

The puppies were picked up again and examined from top to toe. They were all equally pretty. One was ginger and white, the other two were brindled like their mother. They all had thick, soft fur, big paws, dark blue eyes and floppy, triangular ears.

"I'll have the biggest," the boy decided at last, picking up his choice, one of the brindled puppies. "It's a boy, too, and I'm going to call him Bruno. My father used to have a dog called Bruno. He used to take it hunting."

Bruno was carried home. The other two puppies were left among the rubble behind the houses, where the boys had finally stopped and made their decision. They had tired of carrying them around and some were a bit doubtful about the mysterious disease Luisito's aunt had died of. Now their main interest was to see what Alberto's father would think of Bruno, and to keep on good terms with Alberto so that from time to time he would let them share the dog with him.

Alberto's cottage had chickens, a duck, two rabbits, a turkey and a host of cats living among the eaves and grapevine. His parents had come to the city from the country and were used to having animals about the place. His mother was suitably impressed by Bruno's appearance, filled an old plastic dish with milk, told Alberto to tie

19

the puppy to the tree in the patio and not let his friends make too much fuss of it.

"Animals don't like to be bothered," she told him, pushing a couple of rags into his arms. "Now put those down for him to sleep on and when your father comes home we'll get him to fix up some kind of kennel for him."

So Bruno was given the milk and the rags, and a string was tied around his neck and fastened to a nail in the tree trunk. The boys sat around him, taking it in turns to stroke him and let him nibble their fingers, and Bruno was happy enough because his belly was filled at last and he had all the attention he needed.

2

That night it rained, a cloudburst at first followed by an endless, insidious drizzle that soaked everything. The mother dog returned to her shelter at the ruined cottage but knew as soon as she crossed the threshold that the puppies were no longer there.

However, she sniffed about for them and even called to them with a few sharp barks, tail tip twitching expectantly. Her thick coat was sodden with rain and after a few questing circles about the broken walls, she gave up looking for them. She went back to the comparative dryness of her shelter, shook herself briskly, then curled up in the cupboard where so recently her puppies had huddled into her, and fell asleep.

Now and again her eyes opened and she changed her position with a sigh and when the morning came, gray and drizzling still, she trotted away from the place and returned no more.

That same night Bruno, tied beneath the tree, comfortable at first among his rags and empty plastic dish, began to whimper when he found himself alone. The lights had all gone out, the patio was in darkness, the only sounds were those of the rabbits and the cats gliding along the branches over his head. He missed the boy who had played with him all evening but most of all he missed the closeness and the warmth of his lost sisters.

He sucked at the rags for a while, he sucked at his own brindle paws, and he chewed the rim of the plastic plate, but his loneliness grew more pressing and he began to whimper sorrowfully. Nothing pleasant resulted from his cries for it was at that moment that the rain suddenly poured down and drenched him.

He sprang up, fell flat on his chin as the rope dragged him off balance, forcing a flurry of terrified yelps out of him. The door of the cottage opened. Alberto came rushing out and pulled him into his arms.

"Poor little thing. You're getting wet, aren't you? Wait a minute while I get the string untied and I'll take you inside."

Bruno pushed his blunt muzzle beneath Alberto's arm, his stumpy legs scrabbling at the jersey, and soon he was inside the cottage, being dried with an old towel, another plateful of milk pushed in front of him, with several voices exclaiming about him in agreeable tones.

That night, while the rain endlessly fell, Bruno slept with his nose tucked against Alberto's chest, covered with sheet and blanket, lulled by the rhythmic beating of the boy's heart which sounded just like his mother's.

At the same time two little puppies, lost among the piles of junk and rubble on the empty plain, huddled together whimpering, cold, hungry, soaking wet, with mud sticking to their chubby legs and furry tails. They had found nothing to eat all day except a dead cockroach which had been too tough for them, and they had completely lost their sense of direction.

The cottages were not so very far away but their tired little legs had failed them. Besides, they had no particular reason for wanting to reach them and waited helplessly among the cinders and brick dust for their mother to come and find them. The rain splashed on their noses, flooded their eyes, flattened their fur, and when their throats ached from useless yelping they fell silent and tried to sleep.

The ginger-and-white puppy that had followed the women from the fountain was faring better, if not so well as Bruno. Manolo had lost his heart to the little animal and was determined to keep her, in spite of his mother's reaction.

For a long time he had nursed the little thing in his arms, letting her suck hungrily at his jersey until she had fallen asleep, and then he had wandered about with her, vaguely, wondering how and where he could keep her without his mother finding out.

"Lindita, Lindita," he crooned to her, which means "little pretty one" and is a very common name for dogs, and he buried his nose into her soft white chest, delighting in her sweet smell and not noticing the fleas that ran about all over her.

He roamed all around the rows of cottages without finding a suitable hiding place. He saw the seven boys, one of them holding a puppy, but kept away from them, afraid that they might want to take his Lindita away. It didn't occur to him that the two puppies might be of the same litter because they were so different in coloring. Besides, there was only one thought in his mind —to find a safe hiding place for his dog.

At last he stopped in front of a big, broken crate, which had ended its days here after carrying broiler chickens to the slaughterhouse year after year. The bars were thickly stained with chicken droppings and wisps of white feathers. It would make a big enough cage for the little puppy. It would keep her from wandering away, but it would hardly keep her warm and dry.

Manolo pushed the puppy beneath the crate.

She sat there quite contentedly, licking her jaws, while the boy searched about for something with which to cover the open slats. He dragged a large plastic bag from a rubbish heap, which had once covered a new mattress. It was strong, though broken in places and dirty, and he draped it over the crate, weighing it down with bits of brick and tiles. He found half a chair and dumped it on the top and when he'd finished he was certain that the plastic wouldn't blow away.

Then he pulled Linda out of the crate again and put her back in his arms.

"I'll look after you," he told her. "I'm going to get you something to eat now. You'll see."

He had a peseta in his pocket and went with the puppy to the bread shop and bought a bun, which he broke into little pieces and fed to her. Loud shrieks of "Manolo! Manolo!" echoed along all the alleys. That was his mother calling.

Regretfully he pushed the puppy back into the crate, closed up the entrance with a few broken bricks and promised to come back later.

He did come back and the ginger-and-white puppy spent most of the afternoon in his arms. She was hungry but Manolo had no more pesetas to spend. He gave her some of his bread and chocolate. He took her to the fountain and let her drink and when the sun began to sink behind the hilly piles of rubble, he heard his mother calling again and had to leave her.

For a while the puppy slept, whimpering subconsciously for her mother, for the satisfaction of a dug to pull at, and she was awakened from her dreams by the rush of rain beating on the plastic above her head. She flattened herself to the earth, terrified by the sound, and soon the water found its way through the gaps in the plastic. The dry earth turned to mud, the shelter so carefully prepared by Manolo harbored a dozen fast-running rivulets from which the puppy couldn't escape however she tried.

In the end she curled up in one of the corners and endured the rain, but there was no more sleep and no more comforting dreams. Hunger gnawed inside her, she shivered with damp and cold, and she was even too miserable to cry.

3

Boys

1

By the time Manolo awoke the next morning the drizzle had been dispersed by a blustery wind, at times noisy and violent, at times hardly more than a whisper. It was Sunday and as soon as he had pulled on his clothes and swallowed the coffee and biscuits that were his usual breakfast, he rushed out of the cottage. His mother's exhortations about his uncombed hair and dirty face fell on heedless ears. There was only one thought in his mind, only one sensation in all his being—worry and love for the puppy he had found the day before.

He didn't notice the puddles and mud in which he had to kneel in order to drag the little animal from the hiding place and only became aware of them when he saw her bedraggled appearance. Her fluffy white chest was stiff with dirt; her nose, her head, her rump were smudged all over, while the four, scrabbling little paws streaked his face and jersey with long, earthy stripes.

How she yelped and cried and whimpered when she saw him! Her claws scratched his neck, her tongue and dirty nose half blinded him as they blundered into his eyes. She squirmed and wriggled so much that he could hardly keep hold of her and he suddenly sat back in the mud as he lost his balance beneath her exuberant attack on him. He could hardly speak with the joy of her greeting and his heart felt as though it would burst with delight.

"Enough! Enough!" he cried at last, although he didn't really mind in the slightest. And he let her lick and slobber over him a bit longer, until he suddenly realized what a filthy state he was in.

He jumped up and put her down where the ground was drier; then he started walking, looking back at the nonplussed little animal, involuntarily grinning at the hurt expression which had come over her.

"Come on," he urged, clicking his fingers. "Come on."

Suddenly delighted again, she bounded after him in small, frolicking leaps, her white-tipped tail waving. As Manolo went along admiring her, walking backward so that he needn't take his eyes off her and snapping his fingers to keep her going, another boy came up. He was older than Manolo and something of a bully.

"Is she yours?" he said, jerking his head in the direction of the puppy.

"Yes."

"How long have you had her then?"

"Since yesterday," and he pulled the puppy into his arms in proof of possession.

"Let's have her."

"No. She's mine."

"I bet she's not, really. Who gave her to you?"

"My father brought her home from work for me yesterday."

"You're a liar. Alberto's got one, too, and he said he found it. He said there were three of them and that I could have one if I could find them."

"I don't know anything about Alberto's puppy. But this one's mine and you're not having it."

He broke into a run, half afraid that the other boy would snatch the puppy from his arms, and in a moment he was outside his home, the boy not far behind, watching him. He couldn't leave the puppy outside. She mightn't be there when he came out again. But how could he take her in?

For a moment he hesitated. The boy was grinning and in no hurry to go away. In the end he thought it best to risk his mother's disapproval. If she were in a good mood she mightn't mind him bringing the puppy home. He'd forgotten about his sister, though. She was terrified of dogs, even tiny ones, and gave a scream just as soon as he closed the door behind him.

29

"Mama! Mama!" she screeched.

"Shut up," snapped Manolo. "She won't hurt you. She's only a puppy."

He felt like pushing his sister off the chair she was hugging. She was always spoiling everything for him. His mother came rushing into the room, still in dressing gown and hair curlers, ready to tear apart whoever had made her darling baby scream in such a way.

"Manolo! What did I say about that animal yesterday! Get it out of here. How on earth could you think of bringing it in here? And look what you've done to your sister! Never mind, darling." She pulled the small girl into her arms. "We'll soon get rid of that horrible brute. Manolo! Outside with it at once. And just look at the state you're in! Just you wait till I get hold of you."

Manolo slunk outside and shut the door. The boy was still there. He'd undoubtedly heard his mother's outburst. Everyone must have heard it.

"I'll have it," he offered again, holding out his arms.

Manolo hugged the puppy close. "Go and find yourself another one. She's mine and you're not having her."

The boy laughed but at least he went away and Manolo wandered off in the opposite direction, miserable, feeling cold now, wondering what he could do. The puppy struggled in his arms and whimpered.

"I bet you're hungry," he said. "I would have

given you something to eat, but you can see what my mother's like. If it'd been my sister who'd found you, that might have been a different story."

He sat down on a chunk of tumbled masonry, keeping the puppy on his lap. His brooding expression became smiles as the little animal started to suck his fingers. She sucked with such force that she almost hurt him.

"You're really hungry!" he exclaimed, and his brow creased with worry. Where could he find her something to eat?

Manolo knew very little about dogs, except that he had always wanted one and had always

been denied. He knew they ate bones when they were grown up but supposed that this little thing, with such pinpricks for teeth, wouldn't be able to manage anything so hard. But what could he give her? He had no money today with which to buy her a bun and vaguely realized that what she really wanted was milk. It was no good asking his mother for any. . . .

A smile dispersed his frown as an idea came to him. He stood up.

First of all he would take Linda back to her hiding place. He was afraid to leave her where that boy might find her. Later on he would find some better place to keep her but just now there wasn't time. She began to whine just as soon as he pushed her back into the crate.

He ran back to his neighbor's house, knocked at the door and when the woman answered, said, "My mother says could you lend her a cup full of milk until she has time to go to the dairy? She just wants enough for her coffee."

Within a minute the cup of milk was in his hands and there was a handful of biscuits stuffed in his pocket, too. The neighbor was a bit awkward when she stood in the doorway to watch that he didn't spill it on the way to his own home, but after hesitating long enough, she went away.

Carefully he carried the cupful of milk back to Linda, eagerly anticipating her pleasure. Some of it he spilled on the way but there was plenty for the puppy. He pulled her out of the hiding place, sat her on his knees, and let her stick her nose in the cup.

She didn't know how to lap it up properly, although the smell of it sent her into a frenzy of hungered excitement. She got it up her nose and in her eyes and over Manolo's knees but hardly any at all in her stomach until it occurred to Manolo that he must give it to her on his fingers. Like that she managed to suck it down but it wasn't really enough to satisfy her. He crumbled the biscuits, wishing he'd thought of mixing them up with the milk like his mother used to do for his sister when she was a baby. But it was too late now.

The puppy managed to chew them up, after spitting them out several times. By the time the meal was over, Manolo was sticky with milk and soggy biscuit remains and he could hear his mother shrieking his name.

"Manolo! Manolo! Where is that boy? When I see him . . . Manolo!"

With a regretful sigh, he decided that he would have to go. He probably had to get ready for Mass, which meant changing into his suit and a white shirt with a bow tie.

"You're lucky you're only a dog," he said to the puppy, who was chewing at his trouser bottom with playful snarls. "You don't have to bother about dressing up."

He put her back into the crate, promising himself that at the first opportunity he would find a better place to keep her, and throughout the long, miserable morning her piteous yelps on being left again resounded in every part of him.

2

Around about midday the wind dropped. The sun was shining strongly now and it gave a sense of warmth and comfort to the two puppies still huddled together among the mounds of rubble. When not sleeping they had spent the time sucking each other with growing frustration and now that they began to feel warmer, they also felt a new urge to explore.

The brindle puppy moved first. She didn't frolic and gambol as she had done the day before. Her movements were shaky and two or three times she sat back involuntarily on her haunches, almost falling over. The ginger-and-white puppy watched her for a while then, not wanting to be alone, began to follow.

They crept forward, noses close to the ground, but there was nothing but brick dust, twisted metal and rotting paper about them. The paper was easiest for the tiny teeth but it wasn't exactly palatable, even in their hunger, and after a few mouthfuls they searched for something better.

There was nothing.

They kept going until their weak condition forced them to rest and still all about them were

mounds of rubble and rubbish and nothing else.
The cottages were about a quarter of a mile
away and the puppies could hear the sound of
people. They heard the barking of dogs, the
crowing of a cock, but they could see none of
these things because they were far too small to
lift their gaze much beyond the level of a couple
of bricks.

The ginger-and-white puppy crawled beneath
a rotting car seat and curled herself up to sleep
again. She snarled at her brindle sister who tried
to share the space with her, and was left alone.
The second puppy wandered on a little farther,
coming to a crack in the ground which was lined
with a few blades of grass and wild flowers. A
trickle of water drew her attention and at this
she lapped, after half choking herself before
realizing how to use her tongue, and then she
curled up on a patch of grass that had dried in
the sun and fell asleep.

It was there that Carlos found her later that
afternoon. He lived in a block of flats beyond
the cottages and had wandered that way out of
sheer curiosity and boredom. He was too new to
the district to have made friends, so time lay
heavy on his hands that Sunday afternoon. He
was thirteen, too young according to his sixteen-
year-old brother to share his pursuits; lonely.

He found the crack in the ground along which
the narrow, dirty stream trickled and because

there was a little bit of grass and a few flowers, he thought there might be frogs or lizards or something. When he first saw the brindle puppy he thought she was dead, but then he saw the tiny flanks heave and picked her up, his heart jumping with excitement at his find.

The deserted place, her bedraggled condition, made him sure that she belonged to no one. He pushed her inside his jacket and turned for home, his instinct being to get away from the place as soon as possible, just in case someone came for her.

Within twenty minutes he had the little creature laid out on a cloth on the kitchen floor, his parents sharing his anxiety about her pitiful state.

"Do you think she'll live?" he asked.

"Perhaps," answered his father. "It's too soon to tell. She seems very weak at the moment."

"Nothing that warmth and good feeding won't cure," said his mother confidently.

"I can keep her, can't I?" said Carlos, looking from one to the other.

"I don't know whether we're allowed to keep animals in these flats," his father began, but his mother interrupted sharply. "The rest of the neighbors can say what they like. This is our home and we can keep a dog in it if we want to."

Carlos grinned and chucked the brindle puppy under the chin. His fingers guided her to the dish of warm bread and milk which his mother had prepared but she didn't seem to want very much and most of it dribbled from her jaws.

"Let her sleep," his mother suggested. "We'll put her in the box they brought the television in, with a hot-water bottle, and you'll see how tomorrow she'll be much better."

The puppy slept with an old blanket wrapped around her and the tall sides of the television box keeping in the warmth exuded by the hot-water bottle. Carlos sat on the floor beside her for most of the evening. Every now and again he stroked her gently but she hardly stirred. When his brother came home they shared the vigil, passing the long hours talking about all the things they would do with her as soon as she was better, arguing about a name.

Their mother came back from a visit to her neighbor with a baby's bottle, which she half filled with a mixture of milk, water, sugar and a teaspoonful of brandy.

"Try giving her this, Carlos," she said. "Perhaps she'll manage to swallow better if she only has to suck the teat."

He cradled her in his arms as if she were a baby, and had to force the jaws apart to get the teat into her mouth. At first the milk began to drip down onto his jersey again but all of a sudden she seemed to realize that this was food, that this was what she had been needing for so long, and in no time at all the bottle was empty.

"Let me give her some more," he cried delightedly, but his mother shook her head.

"It's best to wait for a couple of hours. If she's had nothing in her stomach all this time we might do her more harm than good by overfilling it now."

So Carlos put her back to sleep in the box, after nursing her a while longer to give his mother time to replace the water in the bottle, and at midnight his brother took a turn at feeding her, watched anxiously by Carlos who was certain he wouldn't be able to do it as well as he had.

But the puppy swallowed everything to the last drop and now she woke up and wanted to play. She scratched the boys' hands with her teeth. She made them laugh with her fumbling walk and tiny wagging tail, her sharp efforts at barking. Very soon she was tired again and they put her back in her nest. Carlos had the box by his bed all night and fell asleep with his hands resting on her blanket-covered back.

That night it rained again. The ginger-and-white puppy under the car seat didn't get wet. It was almost warm there. The car seat had been there for a long time and the ground was dry and earthy.

She had woken up and, finding herself alone, cried for a long time. Except for the steady beat of the rain on the worn leather above her, there was no answering sound. When she was weary with yelping and whimpering, she tucked her nose into her flank and once more fell asleep. As the night went by the warmth dissipated and, by morning, she was as frozen as the ground upon which she lay.

4

Two Little Dogs

1

A week went by, during which time Carlos and his brother grew to love the tiny puppy equally well. They quarreled over a name for her, Carlos insisting on the right to choose it himself as he had found her, but in the end their mother solved the problem by constantly calling her Chiquita—Little Girl—at which sound she was immediately alert.

Both boys were out all day at school so that Chiquita, when she wasn't sleeping, followed their mother about everywhere, getting under her feet and yelping when she was trodden on, but doing the same thing again only a few minutes later. The mother put her in the television box to keep her out of the way but Chiquita cried so much until she learned how to get out of it by herself that it was impossible to escape her demands for attention.

She seemed strong and healthy in spite of the condition in which Carlos found her. They fed her with care on baby food, milk and finely chopped meat and they didn't take her down to the street because their mother said she should be vaccinated first.

"When is she going to be vaccinated then?" asked Carlos impatiently, longing to have her romping at his side or chasing after sticks.

"Just as soon as she's a little bigger and a little stronger."

One morning when Carlos got out of bed and went to Chiquita's box, which was the first thing he always did, she didn't seem to be so pleased as usual at the sight of him. She took hardly any notice of his tickling fingers and tucked her black muzzle back into her flank again, wanting to go on sleeping.

"Chiquita. Chiquita. What's the matter?'" the boy asked anxiously and he pulled her into his arms.

Her nose was hot and dry.

"Leave her," suggested his mother after having a close look at her. "Perhaps she just feels a bit off-color, the same as humans do sometimes. It's best to leave her alone if she's not feeling well. I expect by the time you come home this afternoon she'll be all right."

She seemed to get a bit better although she was very snuffly and did little playing and adventuring that day, straying about the flat with tucked-up appearance and not even complaining when the woman put her back in her box and covered her over with an old jersey.

Carlos wanted to have her sleeping on his bed that night but his mother wouldn't let him. "You can have the box by your bed but that's all."

He watched her for a long time, as did his brother, but although they could tell that she wasn't really well, neither could say she looked very ill. She slept all night and woke the next day with runny ears as well as a runny nose. She didn't want anything to eat at all, not even her milk which normally she loved.

"She's ill," insisted Carlos. "She's very ill."

"It looks like it," his mother sadly agreed.

"But what's the matter with her? She was all right the other day."

His mother shook her head. She didn't know. "I'll try to find a vet and see what he says. I only hope he doesn't charge too much."

There were no vets in that part of the city. Hardly anyone kept dogs and the vets listed in the telephone book lived in very expensive districts and were hardly likely to be interested in a sickly stray. She did what she could, keeping her warm, keeping her clean, and suffering for Carlos who had grown to love her so much in so short a space of time. His brother, in spite of his fondness for the puppy, had many other interests and she knew his affection for it was only skin deep. Carlos had found it, Carlos had lost his heart to it, and she realized that so very soon he was going to be without it.

She tried to prepare him for this stark fact but he would have none of it. Chiquita was going to get better, she'd only caught a cold. How could she die now, being so well looked after, if she hadn't died while abandoned out there among the rubbish? She was going to get better, if only because he willed it so.

He wouldn't admit even to himself the things he could see with his own eyes, her fading interest in everything, her suddenly brittle coat when it had been so soft, the nose that wouldn't stop snuffling, the ears that he couldn't even fondle in spite of his love for her.

Nothing would draw him away from the box where she lay hot and weary. He didn't touch her but caressed her with his eyes and, in spite of himself, he wondered how long it would take her to die.

There was such a pain in his breast at this thought that he could hardly breathe. His mother was watching him and when he became aware of her gaze he said almost bitterly, "I wish I'd never found her."

"I'm glad you did," she answered. "At least she's known love and happiness for a while."

He nodded agreement, unable to speak, and

his eyes went back to the puppy that didn't even seem aware of him now. She was still for so long that it was difficult to say just exactly when she stopped living. Perhaps it was while they were having supper and Carlos had left her for a while. He had eaten next to nothing but his father had insisted on his presence at the table. He couldn't spend the whole time with the dog and although it wasn't until nearly midnight that he discovered her dead, he was sure she had died while she was alone.

The next day he and his brother took her in the television box out beyond the cottages and the rubble. They dug a rough hole with the coal shovel they had brought with them and laid her in it, piling bricks and stones and anything they could find over the finished grave. Carlos trampled on the cardboard box and threw it as far as he could.

"It's funny," said Carlos when they were about to go home. "I found her near here. It was only about ten days ago."

"Perhaps you'll find another one," said his brother, trying to comfort him. "We could look if you like."

Carlos shook his head. "There's no point in looking. You never find anything if you look for it. Perhaps one day I'll just find another, the same as I found Chiquita."

They went back home in silence and when

Carlos once looked back he couldn't recognize the place where they had left her, there was so much rubble and rubbish everywhere.

2

Manolo's puppy was still alive. In spite of her damp and miserable shelter, in spite of the small amount of food he could find for her, she clung to her existence and even seemed to grow.

Manolo had no school to go to so that as soon as he'd swallowed his breakfast he was out of doors and running to find her. He played with her all morning, taking her out on the plain, where she followed him faithfully and romped all about him, her puppy fat disappearing as her affection for him grew. He gave her bits of chocolate and chunks of bread and bought her a bun when he had the money to spare. She swallowed his chewed-up bubblegum and at least once a day he brought her a small newspaper package of bits and pieces left over from one of the daily meals. She learned at a very early age to swallow chicken bones and fish spines and if there were days when she felt sick and miserable, because they were badly digested, there were always days when she felt full of fun and joy.

Manolo was her world. He had replaced her lost mother and family and she looked for his coming each morning, afternoon, and evening as the one certain pleasure of her existence.

Soon she was too big for the chicken crate and again Manolo had the problem of where to keep her until he discovered the cottage where she had been born and the very cupboard which the mother dog had found before him.

If the puppy recognized it she gave no sign. Manolo thought it was the perfect place in which to keep her. She had shelter over her head and it was far enough away from the cottages for her to remain undiscovered, with a bit of luck. He found a piece of string and tied it around her neck, fastening the other end to a nail in the wall. She didn't like this in the slightest, yapping and whining and sitting to scratch her neck every now and then.

Manolo said, "You'll have to put up with it. There's nothing else we can do," but he didn't keep her tied up all the time.

They ran together across the deserted plain, the puppy yapping, the boy laughing, and they tumbled together on the ground, feeling the sun and the wind and the pleasure of each other.

Sometimes Manolo couldn't come to see her and then she would whine and whine, scratching at the string again, tugging against it before falling asleep in patient misery. She had a few old bones she would gnaw at. She had an old shoe that she had dragged back from somewhere and

47

there was the lingering scent of the boy to comfort her.

While she was tied up and alone she would cock her ears to listen to the sound of sparrows squabbling and when she heard the shout of the boy carried on the wind she would sit up suddenly, her eyes bright with eagerness, expecting Manolo to appear.

She was scruffy but pretty, her baby fluff giving way to long hair which would have been silky had it been well kept and had her diet been a good one. As it was, she was continually plagued by fleas and ticks which abounded in that place because of the sheep and goats that occasionally grazed there. The ticks dug their jaws into her skin and sucked her blood, swelling to enormous size until at last they dropped off of their own accord, and meanwhile her skin was itchy and sore and there was nothing she could do but scratch. Manolo would pull them off when he saw them, thinking he was doing her a favor, but in fact he made things worse because the head of the tick stayed under her skin and festered.

She was always hungry and ate every possible thing she found that would go down her throat, often nearly choking herself, more than once almost killing herself, but she was as tough as she was hungry and managed to survive.

Manolo thought she was the most beautiful puppy in the world, with the black tips on her droopy ginger ears and the black spots on her tummy, and the pinky-white zigzag among the black around her nose.

His mother knew he took table scraps for her but she didn't say anything. She hardly worried at all about what Manolo got up to, having already declared him a hopeless rebel, as wicked as the very devil. She bought him smart clothes for Sundays and feast days, she bought him expensive toys for Christmas and his birthday, and she tried to beat him into good, polite behavior. If she had ever been a child herself, or felt like a child, she certainly couldn't remember it and it was enough for him to come with his trousers torn, or to forget to put on his slippers when he got out of bed, or to split his head open falling out of a tree for her to declare him wicked and beyond all hope. His sister was sweet and marvelous and an example that he should follow and Manolo hated his sister who gained all his mother's smiles just by gurgling, when the most he got was a slap around the face for bringing her some roses on her birthday which he had robbed from the neighbor's patio.

Manolo invented a story about the dog. He had given her to a friend of his and the friend let him share the dog on the condition that he sometimes took scraps for it. Apart from this he never talked about the animal, afraid that his mother might one day get it into her head to forbid him seeing it, and as long as he kept out of her way all day she didn't even ask what he had been up to.

The good weather was coming. It was sunny almost every day with only occasional showers. Manolo took his chunk of bread and chocolate onto the plain, needing no company except that of the puppy. It wasn't very far to the cottage but it was beyond the children's usual territory, assuring their safety from casual intruders.

At least, this was the case until one May evening when a crowd of boys happened to pass that way and paused to explore about the ruins. Manolo heard them before he saw them. He was sitting with Linda across his knee, letting her lick all over his face and ears, pretending she was a tiger that had attacked him in the forest and that he was fighting her off with valor if not success.

Linda began to yap at their approach and as Manolo scrambled to his feet the boys seemed to pour down upon him, screeching like Indians about to take his scalp. The boy who had wanted the puppy was there and his expression of surprise quickly became one of antagonism as he recognized the animal.

Manolo didn't move, clinging to Linda who continued to yap excitedly at the intruders, and the boys stared at her, halted in their mad rush by the uncertainty of the reception she might give them. Most of them were half afraid of dogs, even little ones, but the bully pushed forward and threatened, "If you don't make that dog shut up, I'll kill it."

Manolo only tightened his hold on Linda and stepped backward.

Two of the boys pulled some firecrackers and matches out of their pockets. They lit them and threw them at Manolo's feet where at once they cracked into half a dozen sharp explosions. Linda sprang from his arms with a yelp of fear and some more crackers were thrown after her. Crazed by the noise, she dashed from side to side, hands grasping at her, feet kicking, Manolo vainly calling her name. How they all laughed and whooped at her panic! In the end, she dashed out of the ruins and fled across the plain, pursued by the boys who threw their last crackers at her and then stones when their pockets were empty.

Manolo was about to rush after them but the bully gave him a shove that sent him sprawling against the wall.

"Hit me. I bet you daren't," came the challenge as he pulled himself up again, his grazed elbow smarting.

For a moment Manolo held back. He was afraid. The other boy was a lot bigger and was always picking fights which he usually won. He came forward to shove him again and then Manolo saw red. He gave a cry and flung himself at his tormentor, beating with his fists, sobbing with rage and fear. The other threw him to the ground and sat on him, laughing until an unexpected blow brought tears to his eyes. Then they fought in earnest, feeling nothing but hate and deadly intent, until the other boys came back, laughing and shouting, and separated them.

"You wait," threatened the bully. "I'll get you one day. Just see if I don't," and then they all went away and the place became quiet again.

Manolo sat on the rubble, suddenly feeling the pain of all the blows the other had inflicted. His nose seemed swollen and the slightest facial movement made it hurt horribly. It was the first time he had ever been in a fight and, as reaction set in, he shook all over. In that moment he wanted someone close to him and automatically he searched for Linda, needing to feel her in his arms.

But Linda wasn't there, he didn't know where she was, and he jumped to his feet as fear and a new kind of pain suddenly shot through him.

"Linda! Linda!"

He almost screamed her name as he rushed out of the tumbled cottage and looked from side to side, desperately anxious to see her.

There were green patches of weed and clover and stretches of barren, sandy earth. There were bricks and tiles and abandoned shoes, paper, rags, twisted remains of bikes and bird cages among the red flash of poppies and the purple smudge of tiny wild flowers. He could even see ants patiently carrying grain after grain of earth from the interior of their tunnels, making little piles around their exits, but of the one thing he sought there was no sign.

"Linda!"

It was a cry of agony and the tears flooded his eyes, blurring everything.

5

A Home of Sorts

1

Until that May evening Linda had known only one human being and that human being had given her nothing but love and small attentions. When the placidity of her day-to-day existence suddenly exploded around her in jumping crackers, kicking feet and grasping hands, she fled instinctively, not even remembering Manolo in her fear.

The boys chased her across the open land and they soon overtook her. Why they should want to hurt her they didn't even know themselves. It was just a primitive reaction to her fear, to her expectation of some terrible happening, that caused them to grab her with cruel intention.

When they had her in their hands—hard, pressing hands, completely different from the gentle ones she had always known—her little heart throbbed to bursting point. She growled and yelped and managed to draw blood from one of her tormentors and this one, with a cry of rage, threw her away from him with all his strength. She hit the ground about ten feet away and for several seconds lay there completely stunned. When her senses cleared she staggered to all fours, looking about in bewilderment, and then she crouched down to the ground as the shadow of the boys towered over her.

"What shall we do with it?" said one.

"Kill it. Kill it. It's got rabies. It bit me."

One of them put his foot on her tail and threw all his weight onto it. She yelped shrilly and tried to pull away and they all laughed at her efforts and her cries of pain. They stamped on her paws,

taking turns to see who could make her yelp the loudest, and then the one who had tossed her before picked her up by her tail, swung her around his head several times, then slung her as far as he could.

"And that's that," he said with satisfaction when they saw that she lay unmoving. "Come on, let's get back."

And back they went to the cottage, their adventure with the puppy already receding from their minds.

For a long time the little animal just lay there. The evening breeze lifted the hair on her flank, played through her wispy tail and tickled her nostrils. The sun gradually sank beyond the barren green and brown horizon, trailing darkness. A rush of birds, homing late and calling to each other, woke her but even then she didn't move. The moon rose, clear and full, reflecting the white-

ness of the cottages among which Manolo lived, glinting in the puddles about the fountain, shining on odd bits of rubbish here and there.

Eventually the puppy lifted her head and took in the different scents about her. There was nothing special, nothing new, nothing to be afraid of. But a trembling shook her body from end to end as if the boys with their noise and cruel hands were still nearby.

When the trembling stopped she tried to lift herself up, wanting to get back to her sleeping place where Manolo always left her for the night. But the bruised, trampled legs would not bear her weight and she collapsed, whimpering. Several times she tried but each time pain defeated her. In the end she curled herself up, tucked her nose into her flank and fell asleep, yelping several times without waking, pursued by dreams of fear.

With the first light of the morning she was awake again, cold, stiff, hungry and alone. There was no smell of Manolo, no comfort of the things she kept about her in her den, and once again she was determined to get back there. Her limbs were still stiff and pain-filled but sleep had given her a certain amount of strength and she half crawled, half staggered toward her home until she could force them no longer.

Then she dragged herself along, reaching the cottage doorway but unable to lift herself over the bricks and rubble strewn between that and the cupboard where she slept. She tried two or three times, whining desperately in her frustration, falling over a broken crate and banging her chin on a brick. This last was enough to quell the remains of her desire and she lay where she had fallen, uncaring.

2

Manolo had looked for her until it was too dark to see. He had looked in the wrong direction and therefore had not found her. When he reached home his mother was waiting for him with an angry slap because she had wanted him to take care of his sister while she went to a distant shopping center, and now it was too late.

The slap made his nose ache again but he was too miserable to care about physical pain. He wanted no supper, he took no heed of his mother's endless grumbling and was only too glad to be sent to bed before his time, needing to be in the dark and alone. He fell asleep almost at once, exhausted by his emotions and was awake unusually early, even before the bread shop had pulled up its blinds.

He crept out of the house while his mother and sister were asleep. His father had already gone to work, leaving the door unlocked, and although he could hear sounds from nearby dwellings there was no one outside to see him. He ran all the way to the cottage, intending to search farther afield, newly filled with hope, but his heart seemed to stop at the sight of the puppy sprawled in the doorway.

He cried her name as he knelt over her and she awoke with a fearful jerk, instinctively baring her tiny teeth while at the same time cringing away from him.

"Linda! Linda!" he exclaimed, unable to believe that she could react to him in such a way.

He went to stroke her and a savage yelp broke from her, causing him to withdraw his hand, startled. She continued to growl and show her teeth, ears flattened against her skull, giving her an unusually savage appearance, like a cornered fox.

"Linda," he said again, not daring to touch her, his tone reproachful.

What had they done to her that she should be so afraid of him, that she should so soon forget all the love he had given her?

The tip of her tail moved nervously, as if she wasn't sure whether she wanted to wag it or not, and at this Manolo forgot his caution and pulled her into his arms with an exclamation of joy.

She yelped as he hugged her and so he was more careful, stroking his hands gently over her, looking for the hurts the boys had inflicted. He saw that her paws were swollen and when he put her to the ground again she collapsed, staring at him with an apologetic expression but making no effort to move.

Manolo didn't know what to do for her. He was afraid to leave her at the cottage in case the boys came back again and killed her for sure. He didn't know how sick she was or whether her legs were broken and for a long time he just held her on his knees, stroking her, talking to her, leaning his face against her, as if his love alone could cure her.

In the end he decided to take her home. Even if his mother wouldn't have her in the house, she might at least let him keep her outside. Surely if she saw Linda sick and helpless her heart would soften?

In spite of the optimism with which he had convinced himself, by the time he reached his front door his heart was beating fast with pained anticipation. He knew she was going to say no. He knew she wouldn't care one little bit about the helpless animal. He knew his sister would scream. . . .

As he was about to push open the door, it was opened for him by a neighbor who was on the way out. His mother said she was always poking her nose into other people's affairs but at least she was a friendly soul and Manolo liked her.

"What's this? What have you got there?" she exclaimed, struck by the strained, anxious look in the boy's dark eyes.

"It's a puppy. She's sick. Some boys have been hurting her."

"Poor little thing! Let's have a look at her. I

used to have a dog when I was a girl. Perhaps I can see what's wrong."

Manolo hopefully followed her indoors. At least she was a shield against his mother's usual bad temper and he desperately needed someone to be kind to him and Linda at that moment.

"Look at this poor little animal," she called to his mother, taking her from Manolo's arms. "I don't know why boys must be so cruel. Why anyone should want to hurt such a pretty little thing I can't imagine."

His mother looked and sniffed derisively.

"Isn't that the animal you brought home before?"

Manolo nodded.

"But didn't you tell me it belonged to someone else?"

"Yes, but——"

"Then why can't he look after his own animal? Why should you bring it home here?"

"Some boys were hurting her——"

"Poor lad. Don't be cross with him," interrupted the neighbor. "Can't you see how upset he is?"

"I told him before not to bring that animal home. He knows I don't like dogs. He's the most contrary child I've come across."

But the neighbor wasn't taking any notice of her words. She had sat herself down on a chair, spreading the puppy across her ample lap, and was feeling its body bit by bit. Linda cried and bit at her hands and Manolo hushed her with soothing words.

"What's the matter with it then?" scoffed his mother. "Probably picked up some illness. The best thing to do is knock it over the head and finish it off."

"There's nothing wrong that a bit of patience won't cure," said the neighbor cheerfully, ignoring the complaining tone. "I don't think any of the bones are broken. Just badly bruised. Poor little paws," she said, picking one up and rubbing it softly. "Just look how swollen they are. The brutes! What did they do to you, then?" and she clicked her tongue, making the puppy prick her ears and tentatively wag her tail.

"You just put her out in the sun," she went on, turning to Manolo. "If your mother hasn't any old rag for her to lie on, I'll see what I can find. Put her in the sun and give her something to eat and in next to no time she'll be running about again, as happy as can be."

"Really?" Hope and relief shone in his face.

"You shouldn't encourage him," said his mother crossly to the woman. "I told him not to bring the dog home."

"Oh, you shouldn't be so hard on him. After all, there's no trouble in a dog. There's always a few scraps left over from the table and if you tie it up outside the door at night it won't cause any mischief. I'll find it a few scraps myself, if you like."

"That won't be necessary," snapped his mother huffily. "I'm sure there's enough coming into this house for us to be able to feed a dog if we want to. Manolo, go and get that old rug from the bedroom. I was going to buy you a new one, anyway. You can have that for her to sleep on. And take her outside before your sister wakes up. I don't want her screaming."

With a grin of delight, Manolo ran for the rug before his mother changed her mind. He could hardly believe his good fortune. He placed the rug outside the door and then took the puppy from the neighbor's arms, carefully placing her down in the sunniest spot. Linda wagged her tail. She was growing in confidence again and no longer cringed.

"She's a pretty little thing," said the woman. "Make sure you look after her," and then she started talking to someone else who was on her way to the shop, forgetting all about Manolo in an instant.

His mother came outside with a cotton belt from an old dress.

"You'd better tie her up somewhere with this," she said. "I don't want her jumping up at your sister, frightening her. And I don't know what your father will say. I'm sure we've enough, without having dogs about the place. I'll bang a nail in the wall and you can tie her to it."

Silently, Manolo took the belt and tied it around Linda's neck. It was softer than the string he had used at the cottage and she didn't mind. It was a bit short. She wouldn't have much room to move, but anything was better than having to abandon her.

"You'll have to be good," he told her when his mother had left them alone. "You mustn't frighten my sister or make too much noise. If you're good, you'll be able to stay. My mother's not so bad really, so long as you don't make her cross."

Linda licked his fingers and his bruised nose. When Manolo went indoors for his breakfast, she stretched herself out on the rug and fell asleep, letting the sun seep through her bruised and shaken body, pain disappearing as its gentle warmth filled her.

6

"Get Rid of Her"

1

For a while both boy and dog were happy. Manolo spent most of the day sitting outside the door with Linda, often with a group of children lingering nearby. Some of them dared to touch her. Some of them were afraid.

Alberto came, bringing Bruno with him. Bruno had grown bigger than his sister. He was going to be a big, husky animal, with blunt, bearlike head and heavy shoulders. At the moment he was all long, hefty legs and wagging tail, completely wild and disobedient, causing havoc among the timid children with his habit of jumping up at all and sundry indiscriminately.

"Where did you get your puppy from?" Alberto asked Manolo.

The two dogs were so different, both in size and coloring, that the boys would never have even begun to believe that they might have been littermates while the puppies, of course, had no memory of each other.

"My father brought her home for me, from the building site." Manolo continued in the lie, afraid that someone else might yet claim her.

"I found mine. He's a beauty, isn't he?"

"Mine's prettier," answered Manolo, and it was true although Bruno was stronger looking through being better fed. Linda was a prettier color, sandy and white with black tips to her ears, and her eyes had a loving expression that he had never seen in Bruno's.

Bruno was completely uncontrollable. He never took a bit of notice of anything his master commanded, not even answering to his name, whereas Linda seemed only to live for Manolo's every word.

At first Linda was frightened of the many children who stopped to look at her and occasionally stroke her. But no harm came to her and eventually the memory of the pack of boys, and their hounding of her, faded. Manolo's sister toddled out to stare at her, mouth open, eyes big and wondering.

Once when she stepped closer with outstretched hand, wanting to touch her, her mother called out with a shriek, "Don't go near her. She'll bite you," and the little girl began to cry, more frightened by the angry fear in her mother's tone than Linda's gently questing nose.

Now that Manolo had been openly able to

declare the puppy's existence, Linda was better fed. Instead of having to subsist on occasional buns and bits of chocolate and a mouthful of scraps, there was always a jumbled mess put down for her every day; chicken bones, rice mixed with orange peel or apple cores, bits of bread, coffee grounds, even cigarette stubs. She sorted it out and managed to do quite well on most of it.

She began to look prettier still. By summertime she was four months old, still puppyish with lanky legs and a hopeful expression. Regular feeding had filled in the hollows of her flanks and saved her from the rickety appearance of most half-starved dogs, while Manolo's constant attention made her both gentle and amenable.

He no longer went very far away from home with her, afraid of having his experience at the cottage repeated, afraid still of the bully who reiterated his threats from time to time. Linda followed him wherever he went about the houses, snapping up the bits she found in the alleys, hopefully watching the hens that pecked hither and thither and barking with delight whenever she came across a cat.

Once she had a cat in a tree not even Manolo could drag her away. She would circle and circle, then sit down to patient waiting, and when Manolo got cross and tried to grab her she would keep out of his reach, watching his movements out of the corner of an eye, tail waving, apologetic but adamant. The cat always managed to escape, in spite of her vigilance, either by taking a flying leap to a nearby rooftop or chancing its life on mad flight to a hole in a wall twenty or fifty yards away.

Trouble only started when Linda got tired of being so often tied up outside the house. She knew that whenever Manolo disappeared through the door she wouldn't see him for quite some time, and she wanted to follow him. Sometimes, when there was no one at home, Manolo would take her into the house and let her stay there. She liked the kitchen, with its promising smell of food, and Manolo usually filled a soup plate with milk for her, sometimes breaking biscuits into it, which she loved.

Soon it wasn't enough for her to wait outside for him so constantly. As the days grew hotter, the front door was left open and a curtain of plastic cords hung in the entrance, so that air could enter while flies were kept out. Linda could hear all the sounds from within; Manolo's voice, his mother's or sister's, the movement of dishes, the sizzle of frying and the delicious accompanying smells, and she wanted so much to be inside with everybody that she whined and barked and pulled at the belt that held her.

With the arrival of the hot weather, Linda saw less of Manolo during the day for his mother obliged him to spend the long afternoons sleeping. The sunny place, which had been so agreeable a couple of months earlier, was now an oven from which Linda was only too anxious to escape. Sometimes she pushed herself under the old rug to shield herself from the heat but it never occurred to Manolo that she might be too hot there, while his mother never thought of the dog's comfort at all.

Linda would whine and whimper all afternoon and the nearest neighbors complained of her noise, which kept the small children from sleeping. From then on, every time Manolo's mother heard her begin to cry, she would come out with the broomstick and command her to be silent. Linda would stop at once at the sight of her but as soon as she returned to the house she would start again.

Then the woman would come out in true anger and whack! across her head or ribs the broom would fall, causing Linda to yelp with fear and pain. It took her a long time to learn to be silent with such teaching. She would cringe away whenever the woman appeared to beat her, then start up again just as soon as she'd gone, unable to understand the reason for her punishment and crying in the hope that Manolo would come to her.

"I'll teach her to be quiet," Manolo would plead with his mother. "Just let me try."

"You get back into bed. If she doesn't learn with all the beatings I've given her, how can you expect to teach her with a few soft words? You've

71

spoiled her, that's what it is. A good beating is what will cure her, sooner or later, the same as it'll cure you."

Manolo would bury his head under the pillow but still the dog's chorus of pained cries would reach him and he squirmed in agony, as if the blows had been inflicted upon himself.

When Linda managed to chew through the belt she ran into the house, tail wagging, barking delightedly, certain that she had been clever, and once she had learned this trick there was no keeping her tied to the wall. She was tied with string, she was tied with rope, she was even tied with an electric cable, but the teeth that had grown hard and sharp on so many bones made short shrift of these devices. Her one desire was to be as close to Manolo as possible and as soon as she was free again she would be dancing about the kitchen, barking with joy.

Manolo's mother chased her about the house and the dog panicked, dodging under chairs or under the table, hiding under the beds in an effort to escape her. She hit the dog with whatever happened to be closest and she hit Manolo too, declaring that unless he kept Linda outside he wouldn't be allowed to go on having her.

His father brought home a length of chain and for a long time this defeated her. She nearly broke her teeth chewing on it and her mouth was sore before she realized that this, at least, was too strong for her. Then she started to pull, throwing all her weight against the chain.

The first few efforts nearly dislocated her neck and shoulders but she studied the chain and its strength in her long, lonely hours until she knew it as well as she knew the rug and the wall and the ground she slept on. She spent hours slowly pulling from side to side until at last the nail in the wall suddenly gave and she was free again, bounding back into the cottage, trailing the chain, barking her victory, crestfallen only when Manolo began to scold her, hurriedly dragging her outside.

Three times Manolo's father banged different nails into the wall and three times Linda managed to drag herself free, the last time bringing a great chunk of plaster down too.

"That's enough," cried Manolo's mother, exasperated. "That animal will have to go. The neighbors are complaining. It always stinks outside with her old bones and mess, and flies all over the place, and if she goes on like this she'll have the house down on top of us. She'll have to go."

Manolo begged for her in vain.

"Get rid of her. Get rid of her or I swear I'll do her in myself."

Manolo knew she was capable of it. She told him how her father had killed a dog by giving it a bit of cork to eat, which later swelled up inside it and caused it to die, and his stomach seemed to curl up inside him as he imagined Linda suffocating in such a horrible way.

"But what can I do with her? Where can I take her?"

"See if your friends want her. I've had enough."

Manolo talked to Alberto. He was afraid to let everyone know that he had to get rid of his dog in case his bullying enemy should go to his mother and ask for her. He told Alberto to keep it a secret.

"Don't worry. I'll have her," said Alberto confidently. "My mother likes animals," and Manolo went home relieved, believing that by next day Linda would be safe from his mother's temper but close enough for him to play with her every day.

Next morning, however, Alberto glumly shook his head and reported failure. His mother was already fed up with Bruno, who did nothing but frighten other animals and all the neighboring children.

"She says if I don't keep him tied up she's going to get rid of him, too."

"What can I do with her then?" Manolo asked, not really caring about Bruno and too anxious about Linda to pretend otherwise.

"The best thing is to take her a long way off and then lose her. Someone will take a fancy to her, I bet, and even if she doesn't find someone, there's always plenty for a dog to eat from all the trash cans."

"But she might get run over," Manolo objected.

"Bah! Dogs don't get run over. They're too clever for that. And anyway, your mother's threatened to kill her if you don't get rid of her, so what're the odds?"

The idea of just abandoning Linda somewhere in the streets seemed almost as horrible to Manolo as anything else he could imagine. He thought of taking her out into the fields but that would be worse, because there was nothing for her to eat in the country. At least in the city there was always plenty of rubbish and dogs survived somehow because he had seen them. He thought about it for a couple of days, until he could bear his mother's repeated threats no longer, and then he made up his mind.

He would walk with her just as far as he could, distract her attention somehow, then run and hide before she could see him. With a bit of luck, someone would want her. She was gentle and obedient, not rough and unruly like Bruno. She didn't frighten anybody, not even his little sister. He would make sure that she had a good meal before he left her, just in case a couple of days went by before she found herself a new owner. But he was confident that someone would want her. They would only have to look into her adoring amber eyes to want her.

And so, with these and similar thoughts, Manolo steeled himself for the act of abandoning his dog, and whenever the truth sneaked into his mind—that no one would want her really—he resolutely thrust it away. He couldn't bear to imagine Linda with no one to love her; Linda alone, hungry and cold when winter came.

She had all summer to find a new home. That was enough time for anybody.

2

It wasn't as easy to get rid of Linda as he had expected.

The first time he took her across to the new blocks of flats and she gamboled along contentedly at his side, not interested in the newly laid pavements, the sandy roads and recently planted saplings. Every now and again she jumped up at him and Manolo brusquely pushed her away. Was she being deliberately loving that morning or was it, perhaps, his guilty conscience that made it seem so?

He was wondering how he was going to distract her long enough for him to disappear from sight when the occasion presented itself in the form of a dog of about her own age, eager to sniff and play, alone in the street.

While Linda dashed around in circles, jumping and colliding and playing tag with her new acquaintance, Manolo quickly slipped behind a parked lorry, ran across the road, and turned a corner, looking back anxiously. He ran a little way farther but there was no sight of the ginger-and-white dog. His heart beat painfully fast. He couldn't really believe that the thing was done.

His mother would be pleased. At least poor Linda wouldn't get any more beatings. But—oh! What would happen to her now? How could he get used to not finding her waiting for him? How could he? . . .

At this point there was a scampering sound behind him and, as he turned, Linda came charging up to him, tongue lolling, ears flat, wild with joy.

"Linda, Linda!" he cried, kneeling down to catch hold of her. "But what are you doing here? How did you find me?"

If she was aware of his intended treachery, she made no sign, but pranced happily along beside him again, tail wagging, tongue panting in the heat. She looked so beautiful that Manolo's heart clenched with pain. But it had to be done. It had to be done.

Again he turned away from home, walking up and down strange streets, hardly even remembering the way he had come, looking for a second opportunity to distract her. It came when some boys called the dog's attention and started throwing bits of bread and ham to her. While she was hungrily snaffling it up, Manolo slipped from sight, running, not daring to stop in case she caught up with him.

When he slowed to a walk his ears strained for
the sound of her scampering feet. He didn't want
her to find him, of course, but. . . . He couldn't
help listening for her and when she didn't come
he looked around every minute, expecting her,
hoping. He stopped in front of a toy shop but he
wasn't really seeing the toys although he looked
at them. Then he walked on again, hands in
pockets, feet lingering, heart heavy and no longer
hoping.

For a moment, as he drew close to his own
home again, his heart began to beat painfully
faster. Perhaps . . . but no. The doorway was
empty. She wasn't waiting for him. He went indoors and threw himself on his bed, ignoring his
mother who called to him.

She came to the door of the room.

"Have you got rid of that animal?" she asked
and when he didn't answer, except for a tear
which trickled down his cheek, she went on,
"Well, I hope so anyway. It's the last I want to
see of it."

In the middle of the afternoon, when the sun
burned its hottest over the roofs of the little
cottages and the heat was inescapable, Manolo,
lying in the semi-darkness, half asleep, half
awake, heard a commotion in the living room.
There were sounds he recognized, but he thought
he was dreaming. Scuffles! His mother's exasperated shouts. A thwack, a yelp, more scuffles, a
chair falling over. Dreams shot into reality and

he almost fell out of bed in his hurry to get out of the room.

Linda threw herself on him, whimpering with joy. He dug his fingers into the ruff around her neck, rubbed his face against her, and when she was still, looked at his mother with pleading eyes.

"Please, Mama. Please let her stay. You can see how much she loves me. Please let her stay."

"She's broken a plate and nearly broken the chair. I thought you said you'd got rid of her."

Her heart was not in the least softened by the dog's faithfulness. On the contrary. She was exasperated to think that it wasn't as easy to get rid of her as she'd hoped.

"I'll soon make her wish she hadn't come back," she cried and, grabbing the broom, began to whack the poor animal about the ribs until she fled from the house with high-pitched howls of pain. She chased her out into the street, still threatening with the broom. Linda tried to evade her and get back to Manolo for protection, but a couple of hard cracks across the skull at last sent her scuttling.

She was waiting at the far corner of the lane when at last Manolo was let out of doors. She didn't dare to come up to him but half crouched there, tail tentatively wagging. He took her off where they wouldn't be seen by his mother, sat down beside her and hugged her close. He gave her some of his bread and chocolate and spoke to her seriously.

"Linda, you've got to go away. You can see my mother doesn't want you. Aren't you tired of being beaten? I can't do anything for you. Please go away."

She pushed him in the ribs with her nose, wanting to play. Normally he would have thrown stones for her or commanded her to look for cats. Again she pushed, then nipped his arm, making him jump.

"Hey! That hurt!"

She half cringed at his tone, as if expecting a blow, and he flung his arms around her, holding her tight. Her tail wagged steadily. It was always wagging when she was close to him. She licked his chin and struggled free, cocking her head on one side with an expression that seemed to say, What about playing? I want a game.

In the end he went running off with her down the lanes and among the ruins. He went to see Alberto who was sharing his afternoon bread and butter with Bruno. The two animals started to play, wrestling with clumsy paws, biting at each other's mouths.

"I wish my mother were like yours," sighed Manolo. "Your mother doesn't hit Bruno, does she?"

"Only when he gets in the way, and the other day when he pulled my father's shirt off the line and tore it up. She was wild then. I thought she'd kill him. She told my father to take him in the lorry and dump him somewhere. But he said that when Bruno's big he's going to have him to guard his lorry, anyway, so he wasn't going to get rid of him."

"Suppose your father took Linda? He could leave her somewhere, couldn't he? A long way from here, I mean, so she couldn't find her way back."

"But you don't want to lose her, do you?"

"No, but I know my mother will kill her if she keeps coming back. You should have seen the way she hit her this afternoon. I thought she was going to break her ribs."

"I heard a dog yelping," remembered Alberto. "I suppose it was Linda."

Manolo nodded, then went on, "Ask your father if he'll take her. Ask him to leave her where he thinks she can easily find something to eat. Not out in the country. But in another part of the city so she can't find her way back."

"I will if you want me to," said Alberto uncomfortably. He could sense Manolo's distress and hardly knew how to react to it.

In the end he grabbed hold of Bruno and started to wrestle with him. Linda jumped away fearfully, expecting to be hurt, then she came and stood by Manolo, tail wagging, watching them play.

7

Abandoned

1

Linda wasn't at all happy about her trip across the city on the floor of the lorry's cabin, close to the feet of a strange man. The fumes from the engine half suffocated her, the movement and noise bewildered her, and soon she began to dribble and retch until she was sick. The man didn't seem pleased about this, by the way he expressed himself, and she cowered as far as she could away from both him and the mess on the floor, miserably enduring this strange experience.

When the door of the lorry was at last opened she was only too glad to escape. But it was a big jump to the ground and she hesitated. After encouraging her with words a couple of times, the man grabbed her by the scruff of the neck and pulled her down. Then the door slammed, he disappeared, the lorry started up again and, while she still looked about in bewilderment, it was gone.

The street was one of the many hundreds in the city. Its particular name or situation meant nothing to the dog who had no understanding of such things. She felt better now that she was no longer inside the lorry but she stood on the pavement where she had been left for quite some time, not knowing what to do.

She looked back and forth, ears pricked, nose quivering, but there were no recognizable scents. Traffic streamed by constantly. She knew nothing of cars and traffic lights and rushing people who passed her by on the pavement without even noticing her. When someone drew close she sniffed at their clothes. Usually they were unaware of her action although one or two brusquely pushed her away. A little girl toddled toward her, exclaiming gleefully. Her mother snatched her away with the fearful warning, "Be careful. He'll bite!"

The only feeling that surged inside the young dog was to get back home to Manolo but as she stepped into the road a car shot past her nose, making her draw back, startled. It happened again a moment later.

For a while she contented herself with following the curb, unsettled by what had happened; then she stepped into the road again, certain it was the direction she needed to take. This time she got almost halfway across before an ear-

splitting sound made her whirl in fright and another vehicle rushed past her, almost slicing off her tail.

Pap-pap-pap, warned another horn, almost on top of her, and—whoosh! yet another near-miss from those rushing, wind-streaked objects that she could hardly even see.

Crazed with fear, she dashed hither and thither, losing all sense of direction and intention. Horns sounded, people yelled, and at last, sheer trembling exhaustion bringing her to a stop, she found herself in a reasonably quiet alley where there were neither cars nor people for the moment. But even so her fear was uppermost. Though she no longer dashed willy-nilly, she

85

dared not stop, and hurried with head turned back, looking to see what came behind her, blundering into lampposts and the occasional pedestrian, tail between her legs, ears flattened.

She came out of the main road again, stepped into the street and for a second time endured the terrifying experience of being nearly crushed beneath the vehicles speeding in quick succession. She galloped down the center of the road, blind with terror, looking to those who saw her like a dog gone mad. A car caught her in the rump and sent her sprawling but she was up in a second and dashing away, and again came to her senses after running, running, running until she no longer knew why, when she stopped.

She found herself in a plaza where only a few people happened to be strolling. Some small children were digging up the sand with their fingers and a baby was gurgling in its pram. Sparrows were hopping about near the people and these recognizable sounds brought a certain calm to the crazed, exhausted animal. She flung herself down under a stone bench, burrowing her muzzle into the damp, shadowed sand, and for a long time she stayed unmoving, panting hard until all her fear had gone.

When she was sufficiently recovered to lift her head and cock her ears, she was entirely alone. All the people and children had gone and only the sparrows still fluttered about in search of the crumbs among the grains of sand. A slight breeze rustled through the branches of a nearby tree and a fat pigeon waddled among the sparrows, scattering them. Linda watched, unwilling to move. She became aware of a terrible thirst and wrinkled her nose at the nearby scent of water.

She stood up and became aware of the overpowering stiffness of her rear quarters, caused by the collision with the car of which she had no remembrance. Awkwardly she went toward the smell of water but found only a muddy puddle, which hardly satisfied her. Above her head a fountain played, sun glinting on the fine spray that splashed over the stones, occasionally dashing a few drops to the ground. She lifted her head and sniffed longingly, ears pricked, eyes hopeful, but the water didn't reach her, only its tantalizing sound and smell.

She was terribly tired and could hardly keep her back legs from sinking under her. There was a fresh-smelling patch of damp grass under a tree, whose shadow gave welcome relief from the sun. She stepped over the low wire fence that surrounded it and curled herself comfortably for sleep. For a long time she lay there, blissfully unconscious, but was abruptly awakened by a sharp stick poking into her ribs and a rough voice crying, "Here you. Out of there! Come on. Get out!"

A second jab made her shoot into the air and dash away, but she was still half dazed with sleep and her back legs were stiff, so that she stopped in an instant, looking back to see who had awakened her. It was a guard in felt hat and brown uniform who looked after the plaza and kept it free from papers, bottles and stray dogs.

"Go on," he said, waving his stick at her. "Get out of here."

She knew too much of sticks by now to even consider arguing with this one and she scurried away, looking fearfully backward, showing the whites of her eyes. The man stamped his foot and she jumped even faster, dashing across the road into the coolness of a dark, heavily shadowed street, only halting when she was sure the man no longer followed her.

The shopkeepers were just beginning to take down their "Closed" signs and pull up the shutters, the sounds of which startled the nerve-tautened animal still more. Wherever she went there were harsh, unexpected noises, and she spent the rest of the day wandering miserably from place to place, halting for a while in doorways, but invariably turned roughly out, until she lay down eventually beneath a table set out on the pavement in front of a bar. There were some old men playing dominoes and the waiter obviously thought she belonged to one of them because he didn't drive her away.

Grateful for this respite, she fell asleep almost between their feet, lulled by their voices and the click of the dominoes, and the hum of the traffic that never stopped.

2

Although the ginger-and-white dog had never been cared for in the proper sense of the word, at least she had known the security that comes with having someone to love her, someone to love. Now, abandoned, alone, in a part of the city completely unknown to her, she was like a leaf fallen from its tree, blown hither and thither at the whim of a capricious breeze.

For Linda, as Manolo had called her, capricious fortune was now her mistress and fortune was to be more often bad than good.

At first, she wanted only to return to the boy who had loved her but as the days passed by, this intention receded farther and farther from her memory. The busy, traffic-ridden streets filled her with fear and confusion, so that she lost all sense of direction and was driven only to find quiet streets and half-deserted plazas where there was relief at least from the city bustle.

Hunger was to be her main companion both night and day and there was never any particular time for assuaging it, except when the opportunity presented itself. If the majority of the city dogs managed to survive on the borderline of starvation it was because many of the human inhabitants were not particularly hygienic as far as rubbish disposal was concerned. Parcels of rubbish rolled up in newspaper would be abandoned in any gutter and Linda soon learned to rush with delight upon every bit of newspaper. Sometimes it was no more than that—just an old newspaper —but many a time she would nuzzle and tear her way into a conglomeration of leftovers, mixed with floor sweepings or cigarette ash.

The restaurants and bars put out their big cans at night, too high for the dog to delve into, but sometimes she would manage to knock one over. Often enough the rubbish was spilling out onto the pavement anyway.

She learned that during the daytime there was little to be found in the way of food but, until she learned, she passed many days in the direst hunger and misery. Having no body reserves to start with, she quickly grew gaunt and became a tucked-up, scurrying, fearful-looking creature, proclaiming to all eyes her unprotected state.

When people saw her, instead of feeling pity for her or wanting somehow to assuage her misery, they immediately wanted to drive her away from them. Policemen and shopkeepers would kick at her, boys would chase her and find things to throw to her, women would wave their arms violently and utter threatening sounds.

After several weeks of this treatment, shunned by all and sundry even though she might do no more than sniff tentatively at the edge of a skirt or trouser leg, she began to avoid people as much as possible. It was a difficult lesson to learn, having still the memory of Manolo's fondness, unable to understand why one person might react with a caress and another with a kick. Whenever a person drew near her, even if it were only to pass her by, she would cringe, slink away, or even run, depending on what she imagined their intentions to be.

It was only a matter of time before she would discover the comparative kindness of the night, when she could walk almost fearlessly and rummage at will among the human waste.

In the beginning, lost and directionless, she had wandered from place to place but, after a while, a natural instinct to assert herself in a particular place, to be mistress of her own territory, to belong somewhere and know that she had a right to be there, began to grow. The need became more urgent when she discovered that, unwittingly, she wandered into other dogs' territories, searching for food where she had no right to be.

Once, when she was eagerly gulping her way through some leftovers in the gutter, another dog appeared, hair bristling, legs stiff, lips drawn back, a warning snarl in its throat. She only half took notice, too keen on filling her empty belly to care much about the threat, when the other flung itself upon her, slashing with practiced fangs.

Linda drew back, blood spurting from her shoulder. For a moment she hesitated, fear and hunger fighting each other. The other animal, a nursing bitch, twice as gaunt and twice as hungry, dropped her head to the leftovers, gulping and growling at the same time, ready for attack, ready for flight, but determined to swallow what was there before she did either.

Linda watched but dared not challenge her. When the food was all gone, the bitch advanced on her again, teeth newly bared, head to one side, ready to strike. This was too much for the young dog. She turned tail and fled, yelping like a baby, and when the heat of her fear was gone she had the bone-deep cut on her shoulder to remind her of the experience.

Another time she was hazed about by a group of male dogs who pushed her and sniffed her and squabbled over her until she led them into a territory that obviously didn't belong to them, when they halted, looking longingly after her but cautiously deciding to advance no farther.

Eventually, after various similar experiences, most of them unpleasant if not actually painful, she forged out a nightly route for herself, which included several trash cans and a gutter in front of a school where there were usually numerous bits of bread and odd pieces of ham or cake crumbs.

It was here that she made her first real acquaintance with the city's other nocturnal inhabitants, sewer rats, long and plump, usually unhurried in their quest for food. At first she was frightened of them—squeaking, loathsome creatures that bunched together against her when she came among them to steal what they took to be their property—but then natural instinct asserted itself and she began to growl and bite among them until she drove them away.

They always returned, but with greater caution since she had taken up residence among them, and once the most daring jumped up and pierced its teeth through her groin, clinging with determination until she broke its spine with her teeth, when it opened its jaws to squeal in agony. The wound festered, throbbing for many days and nights, and the ginger-and-white dog hardly moved from her resting place in the corner of an empty shop site, whose entrance through a small hole in the facing brickwork she had accidentally discovered. She licked and licked at the bite until it grew clean and by then her fever had gone and she once again felt ravenously hungry.

When she worked out a definite routine for herself, she began to feel more secure and contented. Her body accustomed itself to passing perhaps three days without eating and then gorging to satisfaction on any amount of rubbish that came her way. She found time to stop and sniff at the street corners, to chase after a cat that accidentally crossed her path, and she began to watch out for the passing of a nightwatchman, who was one of the few humans with whom she crossed.

His pace was slow, regular, never failing. He

would bang his truncheon on the last lamppost of every street so that anyone who needed his services would more or less know where to find him, and the only time she ever saw him run was when a clapping echoed down the streets, a client calling him. At first she was frightened of his pounding feet, and the music of his many keys, and scurried away from him, but he never took any notice of her, a sign that he meant her no harm.

After a while he became as used to seeing her as she was to seeing him and now and then, when he felt in the mood, he would click his tongue or snap his fingers as he passed her by. She would prick her ears at the sound, remembering Manolo, and after a while her tail would wag at his approach, while she waited for him to make the usual acknowledgment.

Linda was in no hurry to make friends with anyone. She had learned her lesson the hard way as far as humans were concerned and no longer expected any kindness from them. But this solitary man, with his keys and his truncheon and unhurried tread, passing her by every night, making no overture except the clicking fingers, became an important fixture in her life, part of her territory, like the shop site, the crumb-strewn gutter, the trash cans and the rats.

Of all these things, he was the one that mostly caught her attention. Once her hunger was more or less satisfied, or at least when it no longer bothered her too much, she would unconsciously anticipate his arrival, not realizing how much she looked forward to seeing him until her pricked ears caught the sound of him, and then he loomed into sight, a bulky figure in the lamplit darkness.

One night he said to her, "Hello, Barbas," when he snapped his fingers, calling her Whiskers for the long hair under her chin and she began to follow him at a distance.

After that she followed him every night, always at a distance and only to the limits of the territory she had marked out for herself. When he passed beyond these limits she would stare after him, then sit patiently and wait for him to come back. Before daylight, he was gone, she never knew where, but after dark he would be back, to call her "Barbas" and snap his fingers and let her follow him without caring much or taking much notice of her.

Just to be allowed to follow him, just the fact of not being kicked or frightened away, just the friendly salutation, was enough for her heart to warm toward him, and cautiously she got to following more closely behind him, until she could sniff at the edge of his jacket if she wanted to. She always jumped smartly away when he banged his truncheon on the lamppost, ears flattened, reproachfully regarding him from a distance, and when the ringing sound had died away she would hurry after him again, tail wagging nervously.

8

Winter

1

In this fashion the summer gradually went by. The ginger-and-white dog, first called Linda and now recognizing "Barbas" as the sound that belonged to her, passed the best part of the heat-aching days in the semi-dark shop site, cut off from the outside world by a wall of bricks. It was a safe, quiet place, full of dirt and rubble, unmolested by people, and once she was there any bad experiences that may have befallen her in the street were forgotten.

The feeling that always overcame her there was a good one, the kind that the wild dog must feel when it returns to its den, which it knows to be safe from every enemy. In this place she would chew her paws and lick her wounds, stretch out and sigh with contentment when she came back with her belly almost full, or curl up with nose tucked under her tail, to close her eyes and forget her hunger when her empty belly ached too much.

Here, too, were her few treasures, her few personal belongings. A chunk of pig fat, stiff and rancid, which she couldn't really eat but that she liked to have by her because its smell gave her a sense of security; a dozen bones of the kind that couldn't be cracked and swallowed but that kept her occupied when she felt like chewing something; and yellowing bits of newspaper that she had hopefully carried there on different occasions, their smell leading her to expect something edible within them.

When she came back from her occasional strolls about her territory she would sniff the pig fat and perhaps push it more safely under the rubble with her nose; she would sniff at the bones and paper to make sure that everything was as it should be. Nothing was ever different because no one ever came to disturb her, but she had her ritual, her way of making herself feel safe, and until this was satisfied she would not curl up for sleep.

Only the nightwatchman knew where she slept and even he didn't find out for a long time. It was quite by chance that he saw her crawl out through the hole under the bricks and this wasn't until summer was almost gone.

The summer nights were the best time of all, when the uncomfortable thirst-racking heat had gone and the very pavements seemed to stretch again after burning all day. Most of the rubbish was in a semi-putrid condition by the time she found it but no matter how rotten a thing smelled, or how hard it might be, she somehow or another found a way of swallowing it. If her stomach rejected it, she would swallow it again, and when it at last stayed down her digestive system would often be half-poisoned by it, causing her to spend days in silent misery, between vomiting and sleeping and a general sense of sickness, without her ever knowing why.

There was no doubt that she was inherently tough, for the kind of life she led killed off all but the strongest animals. In her nightly wanderings she would sometimes come across a sickly animal, usually still in puppyhood, eyes half-blinded, legs hardly able to bear its weight, that had somehow crawled or staggered toward a trash can or a deserted corner, hungry still or waiting for an unmolested, lingering death.

She would cautiously sniff at such miserable creatures, instinctively afraid of them, and if she didn't succumb to any contagious complaint it was only because it wasn't to be so.

Most of the dogs she came across bore old scars, new wounds or festering sores of one kind or another. Most of them limped and several had dislocated hips or broken legs. Only a few of them, like herself, were reasonably healthy. All of them moved with cautious, distrustful gait and all were thin and dirty.

Barbas still managed to be pretty in spite of her overall appearance of neglect. Her best feature was her eyes, almond shaped, amber colored. Little remained of the mischievous expression of puppyhood. Instead they were deep pools of want, eternally hopeful, endlessly patient, expecting nothing. Her eyes gave expression to the whole of her tattered, hairy frame that, for a mongrel of unknown ancestry, was unusually well proportioned.

Her coloring was similar to that of the collie, white chested, white bellied, white-feathered legs and white tail tip, and her general appearance was that of the Catalan sheepdog, the Gos d'Atura, except that she was smaller, being little more than the size of a fox terrier. Her ears were close to her head, hardly distinguishable unless she pricked them, which was seldom. With cocked ears her whole expression changed. She became doubly good looking, alert, gently wistful, and the only people who ever saw her like this were the ones whom, at one time or another, she had grown to care about. First Manolo, and now the nightwatchman, for whom she would wag her tail.

Summer, though long, did not last forever, and by November, when the dog was some nine months old, there were days of rain or chill when the sun hardly shone at all. Without her realizing it, her hair grew thicker, adding to her unkempt appearance though somewhat disguising her thinness, and although the wet days were unpleasant, they were hardly frequent enough to make her genuinely miserable. The nights were longer, colder, and the place where she slept insidiously grew damper.

The nightwatchman looked different, with a big open coat over his jacket coming halfway down to his ankles, and at first she was afraid of it. He sounded the same, he smelled the same, but he looked different, and she was experienced enough now to be wary of the smallest changes. He laughed at her bewilderment and she flattened her ears, not sure of his intentions. Then he snapped his fingers as usual, called, "Barbas!" encouragingly and she sprang after him, satisfied.

That early winter she was pursued by half a dozen dogs that invaded her territory, ignored her snappings and growlings, fought savagely among themselves for a place beside her and terrified her with their persistent attentions. Unable to understand her own instincts, which both encouraged and rejected them, intimidated by their demands, she hardly knew how to defend herself.

One night, when a pack of them were about her, the nightwatchman in whom she had so cautiously, so gradually put her faith, charged upon them, cracking his truncheon against skull or ribs, shouting, kicking, raising a chorus of howls and yelps, scattering the dogs in all directions, she among them. She could not understand that his intention had been to save her from their worrying. All she could understand was the hurt he had deliberately inflicted upon the others. There was the smell of blood that gushed from the wound of the dog that scurried beside her, but stronger still was the smell of terror that issued from every one of them.

For some time she was too frightened to return to her usual haunt. She stayed with the biggest of the dogs, who limped from the truncheon blow across his haunches but defended her from all comers and treated her with an affection entirely new to her. He was beside her constantly, nuzzling her neck and ears, watching her. They looked for food together, trotting along side by side, she only reaching his shoulder, and when it was time for sleeping he would settle himself not far away, if not exactly beside her. He had no special sleeping place, unless it was a favorite doorway where he was usually unmolested, and as there was a week of almost constant rain, both of them were soaked and bedraggled.

The ginger-and-white dog began to hanker for her den and her belongings. The wanderlust that had come over her had entirely disappeared. Her fearful memory of the raging nightwatchman was gone and one day, when her companion settled himself in his doorway to sleep, she didn't join him.

She stood staring at him, indecisive, but he hardly even looked at her, his eyes gradually closing, steam rising from his wet coat as warmth began to invade him. She walked off a little way, then looked back, tail wagging, but by this time his chin was down on his paws and his eyes were closed. She hesitated a moment and then she broke into a trot, anxious now to find her way home.

Her den was just as she left it, damper, colder but undisturbed. The bones were scattered in their usual places, the pig fat was really stinking now in a most satisfying fashion—she sniffed at it for quite a long time before scraping up the rubble to bury it in a new place—and then she curled herself around four times and slept.

When she awoke it was dark. She gave herself a good cleaning, licking, nibbling, pulling at scattered hairs until they were as she wanted them, then she stretched, yawned noisily and slipped out into the night. Instinctively, without realizing it, she had chosen the hour in which the nightwatchman began his accustomed round.

She saw him coming, coat ends flapping, keys softly clinking, truncheon swinging in his hand, and her tail wagged nervously. She was suddenly unsure—a flash of memory recalling blood and howls and fear—but his cry of genuine delight, "But, Barbas, what are you doing here? Where've you been?" was enough to dispel her uncertainty.

"Hello, little girl," he went on warmly, bending to scratch her head. "I thought I'd seen the last of you. Come on, then. Are you coming?" and he went on his way, cracking his stick on the last lamppost as usual, Barbas contentedly following him.

2

Around about Christmastime it began to snow. Big, white flakes drifted down late in the morning and by nightfall, when Barbas ventured from her hideout, there was no pavement to be seen at all. She stopped in surprise and sniffed warily at this phenomenon, jumping back startled as its coldness shivered her nose. She hardly dared step into it, disliking the way it yielded crunchily under her weight, but she had no alternative if she wanted to satisfy her hunger.

Soon she was used to it but it was very cold. She discovered that in the center of the road, where cars had passed, the snow was gone, and so she trotted down the middle of the road, grateful for this small relief for her frozen pads.

That night the whole district seemed strange to her. The trash cans had a thick mantle of snow over them, through which she had to burrow if she wanted to find something to eat. She scraped at it with her paws when she thought she could smell something on the ground beneath it, but the few bits were cold and soggy, hardly worth the trouble.

While the snow lay thick and frozen she ventured rarely from her den. It got walked away by pedestrians during the day but at night it snowed again and the pavements were newly frozen over. All this time she felt ravenously hungry, more than usual. She had a litter of pups growing within her and they took from her every ounce of energy. She needed to keep herself warm but the food she ate was no longer sufficient both for the puppies and herself and sometimes she would shiver uncontrollably for a long time, even though she was curled up in her den.

If before she had been thin, she now grew gaunt, with deep hollows between her ribs and haunches. Her back sagged with the weight of the puppies and now when she went out she plodded along slowly, head down, lacking the energy to trot along in her usual brisk way. She spent longer hours in the street, desperately hungry always. She waited outside the school doors and with luck she would manage to snatch a few bits of bread the children threw for her before the caretaker chased her away.

Sometimes she would follow one of the boys or girls if they seemed friendly, particularly if they had something edible in their hands. She would prick her ears and pad along beside them hopefully, tail wagging, eyes begging, and was usually rewarded. But if they tried to pat her she would dodge away, not daring to trust them.

The snow melted but it was still cold. Harsh winds made her shiver. Rain soaked her. The only shelter she had was cold and comfortless but it was the place in which, on a damp, gloomy February day, she brought forth five whelps that had been draining her of energy for so long.

In spite of her instinctive care, the puppies quickly died and she no longer cared for her den, littered with their decaying bodies. She took to sleeping in doorways again, or wherever she could find the most shelter.

9

By the Railway

1

One day the nightwatchman fell ill. It was a long illness and a new nightwatchman came to take his place. Barbas was afraid of him because she didn't know him and, although she watched him and tentatively followed him from a distance, he remained always a stranger to her. He never took any notice of her. There was no overture from him as there had been from the other man.

With the loss of the nightwatchman and her hunger never satisfied, she had no reason for continuing to haunt that particular group of streets. She was less afraid of the traffic by now, having come to understand its ways, and when she took it into her head to find a new territory for herself, felt no fear of crossing new streets or venturing along crowded roads.

That afternoon it was very sunny, just right

for finding a discreet place in which to curl up
for a nap. She stopped to sniff around one of the
big trash cans that were filled during the day by
all the neighbors of the nearby blocks of flats. A
few old bits were stuck to the pavement and road
around about and these she pulled up with her
teeth. The pervading odor of rotting food was
very enticing and she tried in vain to reach up to
it. Someone came with a bucket of rubbish while
she lingered there and tossed it in. A chicken
bone fell to the ground and, as soon as the
woman had gone, she quickly snatched it up.

There was a tree just by the trash can so she
curled up at its foot, unable to desert such a
tantalizing place. She didn't fall asleep at once,
longingly eyeing the big metal container in which
flies buzzed busily, awakened from their winter's
sleep by the sun. Eventually she sighed and tucked
her nose into her flank, lulled into slumber by
the same warmth that had awakened the flies.

A sound of whistling woke her. She looked up
and saw a boy with a tattered pram, which was
laden with folded cardboard and a box full of
hunks of bread. He stopped at the trash can and
climbed inside. A moment later a bit of cardboard flew out, followed by half a dozen dirty
tins. The clattering startled Barbas and she sprang
away, but she didn't go very far, not yet willing
to desert this interesting spot.

The boy's head appeared. He was only small,
very thin but wiry, his skin as brown as an In-

dian's but his hair almost straw colored. He looked at Barbas, grinned, then ducked down again, coming up a second later with a handful of chop bones, which he threw in her direction. Again she jumped back but when she realized what they were she quickly came forward and devoured them ravenously, her hard teeth cracking them in seconds.

The boy went on with what he was doing, looking for chunks of bread, old tins, rags, the sorts of things that scrap merchants deal with. Whenever he came across something edible for the dog he threw that out too, and soon Barbas had forgotten caution, wagging her tail in expectation of more.

There was a pile of things on the ground beside the old pram when the boy pulled himself out of the bin to collect his booty. The bread went into the box, the tins were thrown into a sack, the cardboard was pushed down on top of what was already there, once he had flattened it with his feet.

Barbas sat and watched all this. The boy made her think of Manolo, not because there was any likeness between them but because it was the first time she had studied a child since then. His clothes were ragged and smelled of the rubbish among which he lived, which certainly didn't discourage the dog. On the contrary.

He went on whistling while he worked, taking no notice of her, which was something else that gave her confidence. Had he tried to touch her, she would have fled away, but he went about his business as if she weren't there, rubbing his dirty hands on his trouser seat when he'd finished, taking hold of the pram handle and continuing on his way.

At first Barbas went on sitting there, head cocked to one side, ears pricked, listening to the racketing of the pram wheels on the uneven pavement and the boy's aimless whistling. He was getting quite a long way off, and with him went the promising odor of food and the brief memory of a moment's kindness.

She got up and began to follow him.

2

The sun had gone and a chill wind was beginning to blow by the time the boy reached his destination. Barbas had followed him all the way, never very close, and he had acknowledged her presence by throwing odd bits of food to her whenever he stopped at one of the trash cans. When his pram was full and the wind was already tugging at the flapping sheets of cardboard, keeping the boy well occupied in his efforts to save them from falling, he made for home.

Home for him was in a deserted railway siding, some two miles beyond the southern railway terminus. Above the railway at this point was a district of cheap flats and unpaved roads, ending abruptly at the cutting that sloped down to a high, soot-blackened wall. A well-trodden footpath led down to the railway, which the boy now took, the pram at his back to prevent it escaping his grasp. The cans banged together, the cardboard flapped noisily, the boy went on whistling.

Barbas stood on the top of the wall, watching him, then surveying the lines on which the last of the day's sun glinted. Her nostrils twitched at the smell of grease and soot and that indefinable tang of railways, which until now had been unknown to her. The boy was pushing the pram along by the wall, which stretched for a long distance, growing higher and blacker as it reached a

zone of abandoned factories and warehouses
with filthy, broken windows.

She came down to the track and followed in
the boy's footsteps. There was a smell of rats
and dirty water among the greasy stones.

The tracks branched off into the siding, at a
lower level than the main line, and the boy's
home was a shack built against the sooty wall,
the ground littered with ancient cinders and all
the dirt of the gypsy families that inhabited the
area. As he approached, several skinny dogs set
up a chorus of barks and ran toward him, tails
wagging. They began to sniff at the things in the
pram, circling excitedly around him.

Barbas halted and although she was still a good
way off the other dogs saw her. They bristled up,
falling silent, then started toward her, stiff
legged, muzzles wrinkling, ready for combat. For
a moment the ginger-and-white dog stood her
ground, looking from one to the other, tail high,
hopeful. Then, of one accord, they broke into
the yammer of the hunting pack and bore down
upon her.

Her tail went down between her legs and she
fled, scurrying back the way she had come, heart
panting fearfully, the boy and her hopes forgotten.
For a while they followed her, snapping at her
heels but never quite reaching her, for one of
her advantages was an ability to run with unusual
swiftness. They turned back but she went on
running until she reached the path that led up to

the street. She climbed to the wall, from where she could survey the track, and there she halted, panting, trembling, pricking her ears as she watched the dogs trotting back home.

She wasn't hungry now but she was tired, having hardly slept since the night before and having trotted a long way. This last spurt left her quite dredged of energy and, with the wind cutting sharply about her, her only wish was to find some shelter in which to sleep.

She wandered along the top of the wall, then jumped down to the bank it supported. The wind no longer blew against her and, as nothing better offered in that particular place, she turned around half a dozen times in a spot where the earth was slightly concave and, with the wall at her back and her nose well tucked into her belly, fell asleep.

It was late when she awoke. Far above her the lights of the houses gave a dim glow to the street. She stood up to stretch and then jumped up onto the wall again. The railway lines were hardly visible in the gloom but she remembered the way the boy had gone, pushing the noisy pram before him. She could not forget and her ears pricked as she thought of him.

She trotted briskly down to the track again and went the way he had gone, only remembering the dogs when she had turned into the siding and could see the shacks temptingly near. A big fire was burning, with bits crackling and jumping into the air. She had never seen fire before and wondered at it. People were around it, some still, some moving about, and several dogs were stretched out nearby.

She couldn't recognize the boy at this distance and wasn't even particularly thinking of him just then, fully occupied with digesting the scene before her, not understanding why it tempted her. Generations of instinct called her toward the flames, which suggested warmth, security, safety from the unknown, but the recent knowledge of her own short lifetime caused her to hesitate, to be afraid.

The dogs were unaware of her and she inched a few steps closer, tail gently wagging.

For a long time she watched, unaware of the wind that blew through her hair and bit into her, until the fire went out and the people disappeared from sight, the dogs remaining asleep. Then she felt cold and lonely again and turned back to where she had come from because there was nowhere else to go. She found the place where she had been sleeping previously and curled herself up again, not to waken then until morning.

For several days she wandered about the railway bank and the miserable streets above it. She spent much of her time watching the trains, which frightened her until she grew used to them. Every night she went back to the siding where she had last seen the boy and watched the fire that the gypsies built, too afraid to go closer but compelled to stay nearby until it went out.

She didn't know why she stayed there, sleeping in the same place, watching the rats cross the lines at night, wandering around the streets in search of something to eat. She only knew when she saw the boy again, quite by chance, pushing the empty pram up the footpath.

Overjoyed at the sight of him, she let out an excited bark and dashed in his direction. He looked at her in surprise, for a moment not even remembering her, but she stopped before she reached him, still not ready to let him touch her.

"You coming?" he said, and then he went on up the path, whistling tunelessly, looking back once and grinning as he saw her behind him.

She fed well that day on all the scraps he found for her and in the evening she was tempted to follow him as far as the siding for, by now, she would even let him touch her head and scratch her between the ears. The dogs came clamoring after her again, threatening to tear her to pieces if she approached one step nearer, but the boy shouted at them, kicked one of them in the ribs and threw stones at them all, driving them away from her.

"Come on," he said. "They won't hurt you now. They won't dare."

She looked at him anxiously, her amber eyes expressing uncertainty. When he had thrown stones at the other dogs she had jumped away, flinching as she recalled the stones that had cut into her own body on various occasions, and she wasn't sure whether to trust him or not.

"Come on," he repeated. "Come on."

But she would go no farther. She sat down where she was, closer than she had ever been to the boy's home, uncomfortably close for her liking.

The boy tired of coaxing her. He went on with his pram, calling her once more, and the other dogs cringed up to him and began to wag their tails as he stretched out his hands to each of them. Barbas would have liked to be among them, close behind him, but she was too afraid. The dogs looked back at her but they left her alone and she lay down where she was, licked her paws, licked her jaws, and waited for the boy to come back to her.

The dogs returned and she jumped to all fours. They circled all around her, necks bristling, tails stiff. They sniffed her all over and she faced them as well as she could, though cringingly, recognizing their right over her because this was their territory, not hers. But this time they accepted her, because she had been brought there by the boy, and soon they forgot about her and went back to their usual occupations.

She lay down again, more confident, but when some women came along with bundles under their arms, talking, laughing, she hurried out of the way. For a while she lingered, hoping to see the boy again, but eventually she went back to her sleeping place, feeling safer in the dent in the ground that she had made her own.

10

Nando

1

The boy's name was really Fernando but everyone called him Nando since he had first tried to pronounce the name himself when he was two. Now he was twelve and his most permanent home in all these years had been the lean-to shack in the railway siding where he had lived for some two years. "Home" had no real significance for him, anyway. He had been born to a nomadic existence, like his parents and many other generations before him, and had jumbled memories of sleeping on the ground under cartwheels, of a cavelike dugout in some hills, of various houses, usually abandoned and derelict when not built like this present one of wood and plastic, bricks and old rags.

There were two beds in the shack, one for his parents and the latest baby, the other for himself and his two smaller sisters. There was also a

wooden trunk, decorated with colored tin panels
in which their few personal belongings were kept,
and several fruit crates, which served as chairs
or shelves or for whatever purpose they were
needed. An oil lamp gave them their only light
in the dark and Nando had a long burn on his
arm from the time he had knocked it over when
he was four and set the bed alight.

Another shack was built against their own and
here lived his eldest brother with his wife and
their two toddlers. There had been several broth-
ers and sisters between Nando and this married
brother but they had all died from illness or
accidents. At the time he set the bed on fire,
a sister had been burned to death.

His elder brother had managed to find employ-
ment on a building site, which was why they had
now been able to stay for two years in this same
place. His father sometimes found something to
do but mostly he went out into the country with
his dog, a savage, lurcherlike animal, and came
back with a couple of rabbits, a pheasant or
two, or a chicken. His mother went begging every
day, the baby lodged in a shawl on her hip. She
had some little clothes for it but, when the weather
wasn't too cold, she preferred to take it out
nearly naked, hoping to stir people's hearts.

The little girls trotted along beside her, dirty,
ragged, without any shoes. She had taught them
how to beg and they spent most of the day holding out their hands to the passersby. When they

were worn out they would fall asleep on the pavement. On the way home again they had to climb the staircases of the blocks of flats and ring the doorbells to ask for charity, too. Meanwhile Nando's sister-in-law went with her two youngsters around the shops, where she could usually obtain spoiling fruit and vegetables free of charge, begging where she could. Whatever they obtained was fairly shared in the evening and the scraps were thrown to the dogs.

Nando was almost as independent as his father. Boys didn't go begging and, except as a very small toddler, he was spared his sisters' wearisome occupation. His main task was collecting material for the scrap merchants, dividing it into lots in the evening and delivering it to its destination as soon as there was sufficient quantity.

While occupied in this evening task, he was always surrounded by the dogs who were tempted by the smells exuding from his sacks. He would throw a few nobs of bread to them and, although he liked the animals well enough, he had no particular favorite. The only dog that really belonged to the family was his father's lurcher, a crossbred greyhound, which more than earned its keep with its speed and hunting ability.

The others were strays that had appeared from nowhere, attracted by human activity and taking up residence within its radius. They barked threateningly at every stranger and were useful in their way. They scavenged among the muck of

the two families and kept the rats at bay, while
the only responsibility the humans felt toward
them was in their acknowledgment of their use-
fulness in these respects.

Nando was afraid of his father's dog. Once it
had bitten him and the marks of its teeth would
remain in his calf forever. It was a tall, brindle
animal, all bone and sinew and mean temper,
and the other dogs gave it a wide berth. Even so,
it would sometimes attack them and with one
lightning slash was capable of ripping an op-
ponent open from eye to shoulder. Its method
of attack always horrified the boy, so quick, so
unexpected, so merciless.

When the ginger-and-white dog first started
to follow him about it didn't mean very much to
him. She was a good-looking animal, much prettier than any he had come across until now, but
it was the expression in her eyes that most attracted him; its hopefulness, its doubt, its longing,
its need. She was so different from the dogs he
had lived closely to until now, gentle and timid,
that he couldn't help but be attracted to her
though he didn't know why.

From tossing out the odd bits and pieces to
her, he took to genuinely trying to win her confidence. This was a slow business for, in spite of
her inward longing, the many abuses she had
suffered made her extremely cautious. One minute she would let him caress her head but the
slightest abrupt action on his part would send

her dashing away with fear-filled eyes, and still she would not cross the boundary she had set herself on the outskirts of his home, as if instinctively unwilling to surrender her independence.

Nando had all the time in the world. What were hours and days to him, with no school to think about, no fixed time for meals, and the custom of curling up for sleep whenever he happened to feel tired? He could sleep just as happily as Barbas underneath a tree or in a shop doorway, and was equally as free from most of the trammels of civilization as was she. So it didn't really matter to him how long she needed to grow to trust him. One day was the same as another.

In spite of his nonchalance he began to realize that he liked having the ginger-and-white dog for company. He was used to being on his own for most of the day, but it was better to be with the dog. He found himself talking to her, asking her opinion about things, telling her about his father's mean lurcher.

"Perhaps it's just as well you don't come home with me," he said. "He might try to kill you and then—then I'd tear him to pieces."

Barbas just wagged her tail. She didn't know what he was talking about, of course, but she liked to listen to his voice. She licked his fingers, which tasted of the muck into which he was constantly delving. His idea of hygiene was at a level similar to her own. In fact, he was probably even dirtier than she was for she undoubtedly washed herself more often.

The time went by, one day much the same as another. Sometimes Nando didn't come with his pram. He couldn't always be bothered and then Barbas would follow him along the railway track until they left the last of the city outskirts behind. The fields were beginning to sprout patches of poppies. The earth was dry and warm and they would sleep together upon it, sharing the feeling of freedom and contentment.

Nando set traps for the birds that nested in the fields and he would come with his pockets full of bread crumbs to tempt them to their doom. Barbas watched with pricked ears, sniffing at their still-warm bodies that Nando hung on a string around his waist. He gave her one to eat but she didn't know what to do with it, nuzzling the soft feathers and gently taking it between her teeth when Nando offered it to her. But she dropped it on the ground, not wanting it, too used to old cooked scraps to know that raw flesh was edible too.

One day he found a long stick in the field, a tree branch that looked just like a walking stick. He seized it with joy, swinging it about and imagining himself in turn to be a shepherd, a soldier with a rifle, an old lame man. When Barbas saw him with the stick she wouldn't come near him.

Could she ever forget the many beatings she had endured from broom and mop handles? Even though it was Nando who held the stick and called to her with his usual happy grin, she cringed away, tail between her legs. He began to follow her and she set off at a lope, her whole expression one of fear, and in the end he threw the stick away, regretfully because he had wanted to take it back with him.

Nando thought of a name for her. None of the dogs, except his father's, had names because no one cared enough about them. If you give a dog a name it's because the dog means something to you. It suddenly has a personality. It's no longer just a dog.

The gypsy boy was thinking this one day as he lay in the meadow with her. She had been rolling in the grass and sat up suddenly with a poppy petal caught in her hair. This made him laugh and he plucked a fresh flower and pushed it through the wiry hairs on her skull. She shook it off and it fell to pieces.

"No. No," he cried. "I want you to be beautiful."

He plucked another poppy. She went to back away but he caught hold of her and bade her be still. As always, her confidence in him fled. She pulled herself free and the poppy, caught in her hair, fell over one eye.

Nando began to laugh. She shook it free in an instant but the momentary effect stayed with the boy. She was beautiful and he loved her.

"Come here," he said, patting the ground beside him, but she wouldn't come although she half wanted to.

"I'm going to give you a name," he told her. "How are you going to be mine if you haven't a name? Come on. Sit here. We'll think of one together."

But she wouldn't come until he had thrown himself back in the grass again, shielding his eyes from the sun with his brown arm, sucking an old cornstalk. She wasn't afraid of him when he wasn't commanding her and she went back and flopped down beside him. He didn't touch her, knowing that she didn't want him to, but he said, "Now, what are we going to call you? Perhaps you've already got a name, but you can't tell me what it is."

Time went by and sometimes Nando thought about a name and sometimes he just basked in the sun, like the dog. Suddenly he sat up, and she jumped up too, startled.

"I've got it!" he said. "Karina! Karina. That's a good name, isn't it? It's different. It's not just any name. I've thought of it specially for you," and he flung his arms around her, whether she wanted him to or not.

The newly named Karina sprang away, dragging herself free, and Nando jumped to his feet and ran after her. At first she was terrified and fled, looking back with wild, white-rimmed eyes, tail flattened to her haunches. Then she heard him laughing, and wildly calling, "Karina. Karina. You're called Karina. Can you hear me, Karina?"

She knew that he didn't want to hurt her. Her tail came up again and she charged around him, barking wildly. She had never barked at a person before, either for joy or fear or warning, and she surprised herself with this unexpected reaction.

Nando flung out his arms and danced about the field, laughing, shouting her name, and she barked and barked and barked, overflowing with joy.

2

Karina, as she was now called, had always loved chasing cats but it was Nando, together with the other dogs, who actually taught her to kill them. By this time she had greatly grown in confidence toward him and had given up her lonely sleeping place in favor of a corner by the shack in the railway siding. Rags, cardboard and newspapers were piled against the wall, later to be taken to the dealers, and it was a warm, comfortable place in which to sleep. The other dogs, except for the lurcher, slept there too and they accepted Karina among them because, by now, they knew her well.

It took her a while to get used to the other gypsies but as no one interfered with her—no one tried to stroke her, or even cared about her except

Nando—she came to accept them as she accepted
the other dogs, warily but without fear. When the
lurcher came by, stiff legged, back bristling, she
followed the example of her fellows and slunk out
of his way. He was permitted to steal the other
dogs' food and she let him help himself to hers,
too, however hungry she might happen to be.

Normally Nando never went anywhere with
the other dogs but one morning a cat happened
to pass through their territory and, in spite of its
caution, was seen by one of the dogs, which set
up a clamorous warning, advising all the rest.
The cat at once fled, the dogs on its trail.

Nando was sorting out the junk, Karina beside
him. She hadn't seen the cat but at once looked
up, startled by the commotion. She looked at
Nando, who was following the dogs with his
gaze. When he saw what they were chasing, he
too jumped up, grabbing a stick in his hand.

"Come on, Karina. Don't just stay there! Let's
go."

She was always frightened of sticks and at
once jumped away, but this time Nando took no
notice of her. He was chasing after the dogs,
shouting with excitement, looking back only once
to call, "Karina. Karina."

Halfheartedly she followed but when she saw
the cat run up the wall her ears cocked up, her
eyes gleamed, and she raced to join the throng of
excited hunters. When she reached them they
were jumping up at the wall, trying to reach the

cat which was clinging frienziedly with its claws to an outjutting brick. There was no escape from the bloodthirsty animals waiting below, only a moment's respite until the claws started to slip.

Karina stood with waving tail, giving an occasional bark of excitement. The others were slavering with the instinct to kill, yelping and whining with impatience. The doomed creature suddenly sprang away from the wall in one last, desperate attempt for freedom but hardly had it touched the ground when the dogs were upon it.

It turned, spitting, hissing, ears flat, lips drawn back from its fangs, hair bristling, courageously defiant, and for perhaps a second the dogs drew back, intimidated. Karina only watched, tail still wagging, and then Nando was there with his stick, hitting out with a shout of encouragement to the dogs. With this all three flung themselves on the cornered animal. Yowls and screeches mingled with the dogs' throaty exclamations and Nando's excited cries.

Karina drew back, suddenly frightened. Nando started to whack the dogs with his stick, to drive them away from the cat before they mangled it beyond recognition. At first they didn't even feel the blows so he used his feet as well and drove them off, yelping and snarling in protest. The ginger-and-white dog slunk away, flinching involuntarily at the sound of the swishing stick and its thwack against bony hides, but Nando suddenly called her.

"Karina! You have it. It's for you," and he threw it toward her, swearing at the other dogs as they immediately dived after it again, causing her to run off in fright.

Once more he rescued it from their jaws and carried it back to the shack. Karina hid from him behind the pram, refusing to come when he called. He smelled of blood and violence and she was bewildered. The other dogs still whined around him, trying to drag the cat from his grasp, licking at it when they could, nearly pushing him over. He sat on his haunches where she could see him and deftly skinned the still-warm corpse, tossing the bundle of hair over to her. She jumped away but, after a while, came back to sniff at it.

"That's it," encouraged Nando softly. "It's only an old dead cat. There's no need to be afraid."

The other dogs drew close, whining in their throats, jealous of the preferential treatment the ginger-and-white dog was receiving, longing to rip the skin to shreds and swallow it but not daring to while Nando watched them. He took the cat indoors to put in a place where the dogs couldn't get it. Later, it would go into the cooking pot. Karina trotted behind him, no longer interested in the skin, letting the other dogs do as they would with it.

The second opportunity for cat hunting came only a few days later. This one was cornered on the track itself, where it had taken refuge with its back against a sleeper. Karina was still only half enthusiastic, but less afraid, and although she wasn't in at the kill she did enough barking to make up for her lack of action.

Excitement and blood lust is as contagious as fear and it wasn't long before the ginger-and-white dog chased after an occasional cat with deadly intent instead of her former playfulness. Sometimes the dogs hunted them on their own at night, when the gypsies were sleeping. They also hunted for rats, which were far more plentiful than cats, and they all had their muzzles chipped and their legs bitten. Karina was an enthusiastic ratter and her long-feathered legs and thick ruff protected her from their teeth. She would kill five or six in a night and almost regretfully return to her sleeping place when they were all dispersed.

Between hunting and sleeping and following Nando about the streets, the time passed by. Summer came and the nights were so warm that she no longer curled up among the rats and papers but stretched herself out on the ground, her long hair now a nuisance to her. She felt secure and contented and had grown reasonably plump. She was full of fleas, which kept her scratching from dawn till dusk, and when she had nothing else to do she would chase after them with her teeth, nibbling and snapping, but never managing to gain the final victory.

11

Summer

1

That summer a horse and donkey fair was to be held in a small town some thirty miles from the city. Although Nando's father had no animals to sell, he was looking forward to the event as the occasion for a get-together of a dozen or more families, when he could see again people he hadn't been in touch with for a long time.

The gypsies traveled unhurriedly from various parts of the country, converging on the town with their strings of animals and making a general holiday of the whole affair. Nando had vague memories of a similar family reunion but he had been very small then. The excitement of going somewhere new, of meeting different people, of changing his dull routine, was very animating and he talked to Karina about it, telling her of the fun they would have.

It was decided that only Nando and his parents would assist at the reunion, leaving the younger children with their aunt. All they needed to do was roll up a couple of blankets in case the nights were chilly and put a few cooking utensils into a cloth.

It was quicker and easier to cut across the fields to their destination, but if they happened to go through a populated area Nando's mother would take advantage of the opportunity to beg for some food or money. She carried both blankets and cooking things, while her husband and son walked on ahead, untrammeled, the man with his lurcher, the boy with his dog.

The corn had already been cut and the sun was fiercely hot, glaring relentlessly down on the dry fields. The only sound, except for the occasional cry of a bird, was the constant crackling of their feet over the corn stubble. When a partridge shot out ahead of them the lurcher was after it in a flash and had it between his jaws hardly before the creature could realize what had happened.

They spent the afternoon in the shade of an umbrella pine, standing solitarily in the middle of a field. Nando built a fire while his mother prepared the partridge, which she fried with some rice she had brought with her. Afterwards they all went to sleep, except the two dogs, which were busy cracking the bones that were left and hungering for more.

At nightfall they reached a river, where Nando's father expected to meet with a few of his relations. He was not mistaken and, that night, everyone celebrated. A big fire roared high in the sky and set a whole stretch of the riverbank alight, because no one bothered to be careful, and while the people went about their business the ginger-and-white dog and the lurcher introduced themselves to the dogs that were already there. There weren't many and they were all young, so that from the beginning the lurcher took command and made sure that the first pickings from the rubbish scattered about would be his.

Karina timidly followed him, not because she liked his company but because her attachment to him made her respected by the rest. She tried to keep close to Nando but for once he neglected her, impressed by the horses and donkeys that grazed on the rough ground by the river and, in a manner not dissimilar to that of the dogs, needing to exert his personality among the cousins and half cousins among whom he suddenly found himself.

The dog was afraid of so many unknown people who wanted to touch her and eventually she left him to his own devices while going about her own. She slept at his side the whole night long, with his arm across her flank and his head close to her chest, and now and again she lifted her head to watch one of the dogs scrounging among the rubbish by the light of the moon.

Although the next day she wasn't close to him, she followed him everywhere with her gaze.

Each day more gypsies arrived and soon there were many families camped along the riverbank for half a mile. Some of them went to the trouble of building a rough shelter for themselves from the many canes that grew near the water and the tall thistles that straggled everywhere. Nando's family didn't bother, although his father spoke of spending the rest of the summer there. The chances of it raining were very remote, unless there happened to be one of those quick summer storms, and it was too hot to encourage the necessary effort to cut down canes and thistles and build a hut.

The water was very low in the river, leaving long banks of sand uncovered. The gypsy children played all day on these beaches, most of them naked. Some of them ventured into the water. One of Nando's uncles had half a dozen ponies to sell, semi-wild colts he had brought all the way from the North, where they were only worth half what would be paid for them here, and he let the boy take them to the beach to water them while he gambled with his companions and exchanged news.

Karina didn't trust the ponies very much and she didn't like the way in which Nando devoted most of his time to them. He seemed to have forgotten all about her while he stroked their silky noses and talked softly to them, trying to gain their confidence. She liked it better when he joined a group of boys his own age and they all went exploring together, she loping on ahead, sometimes accompanied by the other dogs.

There were factories farther along the river, pouring all their wastes into its water. Sometimes it smelled very bad but in some parts it was clean, and here the boys bathed and splashed and made a lot of noise. Nando tried to tempt Karina into the water with him, but she refused, and when he pushed her in, she was quickly out again. After that she kept her distance. She was no lover of water.

As the days went by she gradually grew more slothful. The new life she carried was beginning to make itself felt and it was enough for her to find a shady place at the edge of the beach, from where she could watch Nando with the ponies without needing to move. At least she wasn't hungry for there was plenty to be scrounged from all the muck that littered the camping place. In little more than a few days the relatively clean countryside had been turned into a field of rubbish, with food, paper and old rags everywhere, smoldering ashes, discarded pans, broken bottles and empty tins. The gypsies were as impervious to the muck as were the dogs, and babies played where the dogs scrounged, brown, naked and filthy.

The first day of the horse fair approached and the gypsies were up with the sun, tying the animals together in groups. Nando had gone to the trouble of washing down his uncle's ponies and rubbing some shine into their coats with handfuls of dried grass. They were the best-looking animals of the whole bunch and the man was pleased with him for his work.

He mounted a colt that was already broken and pulled Nando up behind him. Nando called to the dog but Karina had no wish to follow him. She watched him go then went back to her favorite place on the beach, restless, uncomfortable, wanting to be alone.

The place she had found for herself was among the roots of a crab apple tree, halfway down the bank. The earth had fallen away with time, or had been dragged away by the water's erosion, forming a kind of cave beneath the roots, which had been left uncovered. The sand was soft and warm and the branches above kept the sun from shining too harshly upon her. She could see everyone who passed by on the beach but was not particularly noticeable herself.

It was a safe, undisturbed place, satisfactory to her primitive instincts, and while Nando was far away, helping his uncle to sell the colts and not for a moment thinking of her, she brought forth her second litter of puppies. She licked them all clean and then she slept, their warm little bodies crushed against her own.

It was dark and very late when Nando came back from the horse fair with his uncle. They had sold half the colts and expected to sell the rest the following day. Nando didn't think of the dog until he had eaten. He ate with his uncle's family now because, among them, he was treated as a man instead of a boy. This flattered him, and it wasn't until everyone had stretched out on the ground to sleep, making a place for him, that he suddenly realized that Karina hadn't come to look for him.

"Where are you going?" asked his uncle as he stood up.

"To look for my dog."

"Ah, leave her. She'll be all right. Get some sleep. We've got to get up early again tomorrow, remember."

"I'll just see if I can find her," he said nonchalantly, not wanting his uncle to know that he liked to have her sleeping beside him. "She's a good dog."

"Do what you want," was the only reply and his uncle turned over to sleep.

Nando quietly wandered about the camp. Most people were sleeping by now and the ashes from the different fires vaguely illuminated their outstretched forms. A baby was wailing, a dog growled as he passed, and he could hear the remaining horses stamping and blowing nearby. The moon was bright over the river but the trees flung shadows over everything. Karina was nowhere that he could see. He bit his lip, then began to call her softly.

He went along the beach but couldn't see her. He spied a long, dark bulk on the sand and, heart suddenly jabbed with pain, rushed upon it, fearing the worst. He grinned to himself when he found it was only a log. But where was Karina?

In the end he went back to his uncle's campfire and, because he was tired, fell asleep. The next day he was off again with the colts and still the dog had not appeared. He forgot about her after a while, because he enjoyed being with the ponies and his uncle and the day ahead promised to be stimulating, and when he came back it was too dark and too late again to make more than a cursory search for her.

He found her at last, when his heart was beginning to twinge with anxiety, stretched on her flank while the pups kneaded and sucked, the embodiment of maternal contentment. She wagged her tail when she saw him but didn't get up, her amber eyes expressing her happiness at seeing him and at being able to show him what was now hers.

"They're beautiful!" he exclaimed, kneeling down as near as he could. "So that's what you've been up to while I was away!"

She wagged her tail again and licked his hand, then immediately forgot him as he found one of the puppies needing her attention. He watched as she cleaned them one by one, pushing them about with her motherly nose and gently dragging them close to sleep, and he marveled at the midget size of them and the way she knew just how to treat them.

2

Only a few days after this Nando's uncle and family packed up their few possessions and made to leave. He asked Nando to go with him and the proposition was tempting, far more so than the idea of roaming the city streets to collect rubbish. His uncle's intention was to travel half the country, buying and selling at different fairs.

"If you leave your son with me I'll teach him to have an eye for a good bit of horseflesh. The instinct's there. I can see it. It only needs a bit of practice to bring it out," he told his brother.

Nando was keen. His only worry was for Karina.

"She's only just had her puppies. She won't be able to travel."

"Drown them. She'll soon forget them."

"Not likely!" exclaimed Nando's father. "Those pups are sired by my lurcher. If any of them are as good as their father, they're worth money to me."

In the end it was decided that Karina would return to the city with Nando's father and he promised to look after her until the following year when they would meet again on this selfsame riverbank.

Nando went to see her before he left. The puppies were still too young for her to even consider leaving them, except to go down to the water's edge to quench her thirst, and her fondness for the boy was temporarily abated. She was pleased to see him but not at all interested in following him as before.

"I'm going away," he told her, gently stroking her head. "I shan't see you for a year. You must be good and wait for me. I won't forget you, I promise."

She wagged her tail and looked at him, sensing that something troubled him, but she was more interested in the scraps of food he had brought for her. By now she was ravenously hungry. He stayed with her while she swallowed everything, but when she immediately afterward crawled back to her younglings, he decided it was time to go.

"Good-bye, Karina."

She gazed at him, puzzlement expressed in her gentle eyes, and she watched him walk away across the sand, leaving deep footprints. He turned back once to look at her, then climbed up the bank and was gone.

She forgot him for several days, until at last she felt that her puppies could be left for a while. Nando's father had come to bring her food and inspect the litter, smiling with contentment at the look of the tiny animals, all of which were images of the lurcher, except that they promised to be hairier. She wouldn't let him touch them and suspiciously watched his every movement.

But it was time for her to stretch her legs and look for Nando and at last she trotted back to the encampment, sniffing noses with the dogs that came to greet her, wagging her tail. She went from campfire to campfire, looking for the boy and was puzzled at not finding him. There wasn't even the scent of him. She went back to the beach and trotted back and forth, ears pricked as she caught sight of a group of boys about Nando's size, flattening them again when she realized that he was not among them.

In the end she went back to her puppies who received her clamorously. She licked them all over, chased a few fleas from their soft, pink bellies, and let them suck at will.

They were healthy little things this time for Nando's father took the trouble to see that there

should be plenty of milk for them. Every day he brought the mother dog a big panful of rice with bits of meat, and when she left them for a while he would pick them up and examine them, pleased to see how they filled out and grew. They were all brindle, with white patches on their noses and feet, with greyhound-like muzzles and long, thin tails. He sold three of them before they had even opened their eyes, taking advantage of her absence to steal them away.

Anxiously she looked for them on her return but there were no clues to their disappearance. In the end she made do with the two that still remained, forgetting the others, which were already on the road with gypsies that were moving out.

August was nearly over and most of the families had other places to go to. Nando's mother was restless now to return to her children in the city, so one day she rolled up their blankets and cooking things, while her husband went for the puppies, and they set out across country again to go back home.

Karina was both frightened and anxious when the man picked up her younglings and carried them off. She followed at his heels, constantly looking up, heedless of his assurance and the whole way back to the city she ran restlessly beside him, fearful for their safety. They stopped halfway to eat and sleep for a while, and then the pups were able to suck while she licked them clean. She was a little less anxious on the second half of the journey, but not enough to take her eyes off them, now and again jumping up to the man's arms, where they hung limply and somnambulantly, like two soft dolls.

She was happy when they got back to the railway siding, which she immediately recognized. The man put the puppies down on some rags by the shack and left her to look after them. When she was sure they were safe and contented she set off to explore her surroundings, instinctively looking for Nando, expecting to find him. The old pram was still there, tossed on its side. It smelled of the smaller children but no scent lingered of the boy.

She trotted back and forth, up the footpath to the top of the wall, nose to the ground, along the track, which smelled only of grease and rats, and even poked her head into the shack itself, ears pricked with wondering expectancy.

She didn't find him and eventually gave up looking, consoled by the puppies that now tumbled over her paws and chewed at her playfully, and tried to follow her. One day one of them was gone. The man had sold it, and only a short time after this she found the nest of rags empty.

12

A New Friend

1

Karina's desire to find Nando again grew stronger and stronger. Though she was used to having no one to care for her, she was an affectionate animal and the love the boy had bestowed upon her was not easily forgotten. She took to wandering about the streets in search of him, following the route he used to take on his rounds in search of wastepaper and rags. The half-forgotten streets grew familiar again. She instinctively trotted from one to another and at every place where Nando ever halted, she halted also, sniffing about, ears pricked, remembering, expecting to see him. She knew she wouldn't find him at the railway siding and no longer returned there.

She took to following every boy she saw, ears pricked questioningly, gentle eyes hopefully gazing into their faces. Some of them laughed with pleasure and gave her things to eat. Others stamped their feet and frightened her away. Some even cried out with fear.

Wherever she went she looked for Nando and never found him, and while she looked the summer ended, breezy winds began to tug at the fading leaves and, as they blustered across the city avenues, there was the bite of winter in them. It began to rain and the ginger-and-white dog began to experience once more all the discomforts of being homeless and defenseless.

If she found a dry place in which to curl herself up, she might not move from it for a couple of days, preferring to go hungry rather than face the rain and wind. She could not settle herself in any place in particular, driven to search for Nando. Even when she came more or less to forget him, the restless habit stayed with her.

Without knowing it, she was looking for someone to love her, someone who would permit her to follow them and offer her a kindly word from time to time. She needed this as much as she needed food, more than she needed shelter, and she spent her whole time wandering from place to place, comfortless everywhere, lonely but ever hopeful.

She came to a mainly residential part of the city, where the roads were less crowded, where there were trees and open spaces and bushes clumped about the buildings, beneath which she could rest undisturbed and even make herself warm among the brown leaves that were blown and swept among their roots. There were cats to chase and rats to kill, hunted without difficulty from among the same bushes that gave her shelter, and occasionally she sniffed noses with an ownerless dog like herself.

Although it became very cold, the sun was often shining and during the daytime at least it was easy to keep warm. One day she happened to be trotting along a concrete path beneath two rows of naked plane trees when just ahead of her she saw someone sitting on a wooden bench, a stick by his side.

Automatically she halted. She was still afraid of sticks and it needed great courage on her part to pass one by. She went on again, intending to make a wide arc about the still figure with the stick, but as she did so the man clicked his tongue, making her look at him.

She pricked her ears, a questioning expression in her gaze. She always looked particularly attractive like this, in spite of her gaunt, unkempt appearance, and the man said in a voice that was somewhat gruff, but kindly, "Hello, little pretty one."

He stretched out his hand in her direction and she withdrew slightly.

"Don't be afraid of me. I won't hurt you. Look!"

Although she didn't understand the meaning of the words, she could tell by their intonation that they meant her no harm, and her ears pricked again as she watched the man fumble with a paper bag he had on his lap. Her tail began to move slightly, hopefully. Paper bags usually meant food and, as always, her stomach was rumbling.

The man pulled out a small loaf. His movements were slow and somewhat shaky. He was old. He broke off the end piece and threw it to her.

"Here you are. Eat it up. You look hungry to me."

The bread lay temptingly on the path in the sunshine. It wasn't more than a couple of paces away from her, but it was near the stick and she was afraid to go close. She sat down, licked her chops and hoped he would throw her another bit. A couple of sparrows flew down and squabbled over the bread. The old man laughed and they flew away.

"You're frightened, aren't you?" he said. "But you're hungry too."

He broke off another piece and threw it to her. It fell at her feet and she snapped it up quickly. Another bit followed and then another. But when he tossed the fourth bit near his feet again she wouldn't go for it.

"You'll have to come here if you want any more," he told her. "I'm too old to get up and go to you."

She listened to him with head on one side.

She lay down and watched him. He ate the rest of the bread himself, taking a long time because he had only a few broken teeth and had to suck it. While he ate, he talked to her.

"I had a dog like you once, years ago," he said. "In the village. She used to help me with the sheep." He sighed and then chuckled. "She was a bit of a rogue, though. She used to steal the eggs when she thought no one was watching. She was a one for eggs was my Canela. If you were my dog, I'd call you Canela after her. Canela! Canela!"

Karina pricked her ears because when he said the word Canela he used a tone that all humans used when they called to her. Linda, Barbas, Karina—they were all different words but it was the way they were spoken that made her know they had a special meaning. And now Canela. Canela was a special sound too. It connected her with this man. In her way of reasoning things it suggested a kind of sympathy between them.

There were only two sounds she really knew well. The one the old man had just used, which was a proffering of friendship, and the cry "Chucho!" (mongrel), which had been thrown at her so many times in the street and caused her to shrink and run. "Chucho!" was always a warning, an exclamation of annoyance, and might well be followed by a kick. Even if there was no physical reaction, the very sound implied one, and she invariably got out of the way as soon as possible.

Her understanding of human vocabulary had really reached no further than these two sounds, but she needed no more in order to defend herself in this half-hostile, half-friendly world: the caress or the threat implied in a name.

Eventually the old man got up with the help of his walking stick. Karina, or Canela as he had called her, watched the stick with close attention. She saw that it helped him to walk. He walked very slowly. He was in no hurry and he looked back at the dog and called to her again.

Tentatively she began to follow him. He went along the concrete path beneath the leafless trees, warm in the winter sunshine, and turned off when he came to the entrance of the flats where he lived.

"If we were in the village, I'd keep you," he said.

She was hardly beyond his reach—just beyond the reach of the stick, and there was that warm expression in her eyes that had so attracted Nando.

"Yes, if I were in the village. . . ." and he sighed. Then he pushed open the door and went inside.

2

The old man lived with his daughter and son-in-law and their children in the city flat. He had gone to stay there when his wife died. That had been three years ago, and although he was among people he loved, especially the toddlers, he was very lonely. His own daughter called him Grandfather. She was brusque and impatient and treated him as if he were a child, only with less love and attention than she gave to her children. His son-in-law more or less ignored him once he had said, "Hello, Grandfather," on coming home from work.

He loved the children and they liked to play with him, but they tired him with their boisterous ways. He didn't really mind about this. He was old anyway and if they used up his fading energy more quickly than if he had sat vegetating in the sun, it was a good way in which to spend his last years or months. But his daughter wouldn't permit this.

"Leave Grandfather alone," she was always telling them, and she would slap them if he tempted them to stay. She never listened to anything he said and he knew she resented having him there. If the children behaved badly, she always blamed him and complained to her husband that he encouraged them to defy her.

One of his small pleasures was buying them

cheap sweets and lollipops from a cart in the street. He would talk to the old man who pushed the cart and sometimes he would bring back a little plastic toy if he had enough coins in his pocket. His daughter would give him a couple of pesetas every day, just enough for him to buy himself a cigarette. But smoking made him cough so he preferred to buy the children sweets. Then she would scold him, saying they wouldn't eat their dinner, they would ruin their teeth or be sick, and he had to give them the sweets secretly and make them promise not to tell.

He had only one suit of black corduroy, a material that everyone in the village wore because it took years to wear out, and although his daughter constantly scolded him, he couldn't get into the habit of removing his beret when he got indoors.

She was always saying, "You're not in the village now, Grandfather," as if he needed reminding, and he wore it until he went to bed, deliberately, to annoy her. When visitors came she pushed him into the kitchen, ashamed of his corduroy and his beret and his toothless mouth, and when the children preferred to play at his feet instead of pretending to enjoy the company of visitors, she was furious.

He got into the habit of going out as soon as he had swallowed his breakfast, not returning until lunchtime. In the summertime he found a place in the shade and in the wintertime he sat in the sun. His daughter would give him a piece of bread and perhaps a bit of cheese if she was feeling generous, and then he wouldn't go back to the flat until his son-in-law had finished his lunch and returned to work, knowing that there was always one too many at the table when he himself was present.

He was very lonely and when he sat on the bench in the sun, often half asleep, he would think of the village and his youth and of when his own daughter had been no more than a toddler who delighted in climbing all over him. He couldn't walk very far or he might have looked for a place where a number of old men gathered, instead of sitting alone. He went only the length of the concrete path and back again, and he threw crumbs to the sparrows and watched the children play in the sand.

When he saw the ginger-and-white dog he remembered Canela, and now this dog became Canela in his imagination. The next day he waited for her. The hours went by but he didn't worry. Time no longer meant anything to him. He had a watch that he religiously wound every morning before putting it into his waistcoat pocket, but he never pulled it out to see what time it was. Time was in the warmth of the sun, in his daughter's scoldings that were endless, and in the laughter and tears of his grandchildren.

Eventually she came. It was almost time for him to go home because he was growing cold.

She had come at the same time as yesterday. He had saved some bread for her. He had to throw it to her because she still wouldn't come too close. But she wagged her tail when he called her Canela and the warmth of her gaze touched his heart.

The days went by and now the old man had good reason for getting up in the morning. Every night he would find an excuse for going into the kitchen while the rest were watching the television, and he would pull all the scraps out of the trash can and put them in a bit of newspaper for Canela. He hid the newspaper in a drawer of the dressing table in his room and he would sleep more contentedly knowing that it was there and that next day he would take it to the dog that would be waiting for him.

Soon the dog lost her fear of the stick and then she came right up to him and let him scratch her head and fondle her ears. He had never much fondled his old Canela. In those days he hadn't been lonely and a dog was only a dog, but that was a long time ago. Now he was old and unwanted, and a dog was the only creature that looked upon him with love, the only creature that actually needed him and was joyful when he appeared.

It became almost a ritual to call and caress her, to put the stick carefully aside, to draw out the newspaper packet and slowly unwrap it. At first he put the paper on the ground and she would look at him as if in gratitude, as if saying thank you with her eyes, before putting her head down to the scraps to eat. Then he preferred to give her the food, bit by bit, letting her lick his fingers clean when there was nothing left before wiping them dry on his jacket.

She was very careful when she took the food from his fingers, never once letting her teeth touch them, gentle in everything she did. The children would snatch the sweets from his hands, almost knocking him over sometimes, and they wouldn't even give him a kiss unless he black-mailed them into it by insisting on the kiss first, before handing over the reward.

Every day she accompanied him to the door of the flats, watching him enter with regretful expression, and after a while she was waiting for him in the morning when he came downstairs and opened the door. The neighbors, who watched everything and kept nothing secret, told his daughter about the dog and when she mentioned it to him one breakfast time, he thought it was a good moment in which to broach the subject he had had in mind for some time already.

"I'd like to keep her," he said. "She's just like my old Canela. Do you remember her? She used to steal the eggs. We thought it was the boys till we caught her at it."

"Yes, and I expect this one would be stealing things too, if we had her here."

"Oh no, this one's different. Besides, she can't steal the eggs from the fridge, can she?"

"Bah!" was the only reply.

"What do you say, daughter? I'd take care of her. She'd be no trouble. I'd like to have something of my own."

The daughter turned on him with an incredulous expression, and his heart sank.

"You don't think that for one minute I'd consider having a filthy animal in my home, do you? You get more senile every day. Really, Grandfather, you're worse than the children. If Ricardin asked for a dog, at least I could understand it, but you're a grown man. You ought to have more sense."

"Please. It's not much I ask for. I'll keep her on the terrace. She can sleep there at night. I'll make a kennel for her."

"And she'll bite the children and bark all day and have fleas. Do you think we're still in the village?"

He didn't answer. What was the point? He knew before he even asked what the answer was going to be.

"I'll tell you something else," she went on relentlessly. "You'd better keep that animal away from our doorway or the neighbors will be complaining. She frightens the children."

"It's the mothers that frighten the children, always telling them that dogs are going to bite or eat them. Canela wouldn't hurt anyone."

"Well, you've been warned. If you don't want to lose her one day, keep her away. The woman downstairs was talking about calling the dog-catcher. You'd better stop feeding her. Like that, she'll soon stop following you."

"She follows me because she wants to, not because of the food."

"Go on with you." She laughed scornfully. "You're not going to tell me it's for anything else. What silly ideas you get into your head now you're old!"

13

Canela

1

The old man was right when he said the dog didn't follow him only for the food. He had offered her affection and her heart was much hungrier than her stomach. Her day now became devoted to the few hours she spent with him. She would follow him along the path to his favorite bench and they would sit together, or she would lay at his feet when he had fed her.

When he spoke her eyes watched his face with gentleness and she pricked her ears. Often he was silent, but his slightest sound was enough to have her alertly watching him.

Later, she would follow him back and after he had left her in the doorway, she would find a nearby brush beneath which she could curl, tuck her nose into her tail and fall asleep.

Sometimes the old man would go out onto the terrace. He would call her name and make her

look up. Then her tail would wag. She was so very pretty with her ears pricked that he would sometimes beg his daughter to come and see her. But the daughter only scoffed and told him to come in and shut the window before all the heat went out of the room.

And this was all the ginger-and-white dog lived for throughout the bitter winter days. Although the sun often shone, the wind was cruelly sharp and the ground was frozen. For hours and hours she would not stir from beneath the bush, with its softer earth and covering of crispy leaves, but even so she sometimes shook with cold. The nights were worst of all, when frost glistened on the ground in the moonlight.

She was often awake at night, listening to the whimpering howls of the nightwatchman's dogs as they impatiently waited for a treed cat to fall into their grasp, hearing the crack of his truncheon against the tree trunks or lampposts as he turned on his beat.

Some days Canela waited in vain for the old man. When the wind was very fierce he did not come. When it snowed or rained he didn't come either and the terrace window was kept tight shut, so he didn't call to her either. When she saw him after a lapse of three or four days she would go wild with joy. She got used to not seeing him sometimes but always waited hopefully.

When he didn't come it usually meant that she went hungry. There was less rubbish to eat about these parts because there were no shops, and most people deposited the contents of their kitchen buckets directly into the big cans provided.

On one occasion when she was ravenously gulping down whatever she happened to come across she got a thick fishbone stuck in her throat. Panic mastered her as she heaved and choked and slavered. She tried to dig a paw into her mouth, she scraped her head along the ground, she twisted and turned and uttered horrible noises.

Some boys passing by saw her foaming mouth, her rolling eyes, her frantic motions and decided she was mad with rabies. They picked up handfuls of broken bricks that abounded there and began to throw them at her. At first, her distress was such that she didn't even realize what was happening. Several heavy chunks stung into her before she became aware of her attackers and then she fled from the new danger, forgetting the bone in her throat.

She crossed a road, fled down a high bank that bordered the main road to the coast, and was stopped by a high wire fence. The boys were still following and whooped with joy when it seemed that she couldn't escape them. Stopping only to scoop up more ammunition from time to time, they pelted her unmercifully as she dashed along beside the fence. There was a hole in the wire a bit farther on and beneath this she made her escape, avoiding a sixty-mile-an-hour car by mere chance as she dashed headlong across the highway.

No sooner did she slow down, utterly exhausted, when she was sick. The bone was dislodged by this action although she was unaware of it. She was unaware of anything for some time, lying as if she were dead on the farther bank, which had no fencing because there were no houses on that side of the highway.

When she came to herself again her whole body ached from the many cuts and bruises the boys had inflicted with their bricks and stones, but worst of all was the pain in her throat that had been torn by the fishbone. She found a puddle and, in spite of her thirst, could hardly stretch out her tongue to lap at the water.

All that day she wandered along by the highway, hardly aware of her actions, plagued by the wound in her throat which set a fever burning through her whole body. The wounds from the bricks were nothing in comparison to this. Blood-streaked saliva drooled from her jaws as she stumbled along, but it wasn't until she was completely overcome by exhaustion that she went no farther.

She curled herself up in a hollow and no longer fought against the delirium that overpowered her. Sometimes she lay with open eyes, unseeingly gazing upon the not-far-distant highway and the almost unending traffic that sped by. Sometimes she slept. She would either get better or die, according to the inherent strength of her body. She had no will or decision in the matter. She just waited.

Several days and nights went by. The wind couldn't reach her, neither could the sun, but the burrow she had found for herself retained what warmth she exuded. As suddenly as she had become ill, she began to feel better. She uncurled herself and stretched and, although her throat still hurt her, the pain was bearable. She was stiff from having lain unmoving for so long and from the various bruises, whose effects had not completely faded, but at least she felt hungry enough to venture from her shelter and, feeling hungry, she remembered the old man.

It was close on midnight by the time she found her way back and, with a sense of contentment, curled up under her usual bush. The leaves were frosted over and damp underneath. She dug them up with her paws and then, with her nose, pushed and prodded them into a slightly more comfortable nest for herself. And then she twisted herself around half a dozen times before pushing her muzzle into her flank and, with a heavy sigh, falling asleep.

2

The wound in her throat was to take a long, long time to heal and, although it wasn't actually painful after a while, it was troublesome in many ways. She could no longer eat the crusty bread the old man threw for her; bones or any similar irritant often made her vomit, and the chronic cough she developed, which was especially troublesome if she barked, was due to the same weakness.

The old man could see that she had been ill, so gaunt and weary looking was she in spite of her joy at being once more in his company, and she picked and sniffed at the scraps he brought her before very gingerly swallowing less than half of them. There was an air of apology in her manner, as if she were trying to tell him that she appreciated his generosity even though she couldn't take advantage of it. She wagged her tail, she took the bits between her teeth, then dropped them again, and he wished he could take her home and coddle her on milk and beaten eggs, or his smallest grandchild's breakfast cereal, until she was well.

He stayed out too long with her in spite of the cold and the cutting sierra winds, which brought flurries of snow or sleet, and he caught a chill that he was determined to disguise, sure that his daughter wouldn't let him go out if she knew about it. She made such a fuss about his health but complained all day long about the work he made for her when she obliged him to stay in bed. He didn't mind about her complaints. He shut his ears to them, but he did mind about Canela and knew that she relied on him for the little food she ate.

The pain in his chest wasn't really important. He didn't even remember it while he was with the dog, stroking her head, talking to her, but in the middle of the second night he awoke with the sensation of being strangled. He couldn't breathe! He croaked for air, for help. Luckily, the walls between the adjoining rooms were so thin that his daughter woke and heard him. A doctor was called. The nightwatchman brought him and when he came near with his dogs, Canela fled.

The old man's congested lungs gave way to pneumonia and, just as suddenly as he had fallen ill and they had had to rush for a doctor, now they were obliged to rush for a priest so that he could die in peace. His last few phrases were hardly intelligible. Only his daughter knew what he was talking about but she pretended to be equally puzzled, too ashamed to confess that his last thoughts had been for an ownerless mongrel when it was expected that he should have had a few words of remembrance for her or his grandchildren.

She was afraid the priest would think him a heathen if he learned that his last, hardly whispered word—Canela—had been the name of a dog.

The dog knew from the unusual comings and goings that something different was happening in the house but she had no way of connecting this with the old man. She waited for him for days, used to not seeing him sometimes and still expecting him to come slowly down the stairs one day with his stick. Now and again someone left her a few scraps but the other neighbors began to complain, saying that the bits she didn't eat would attract the rats that abounded in the district.

The people whose balconies were at ground level, and who had already complained to the old man's daughter, decided to shoo her away. They could have telephoned to the council dogcatcher but it was less trouble to get a broom and frighten her off with that.

And so, for no reason that Canela could understand, every time she curled up beneath her usual bush, someone would come out and shake a broom at her, and even whack her with it if she didn't get out of the way in time. She would run away, tail between legs, and later come back. They would chase her off again but still she returned, and the person most zealous in pursuit of her was the old man's daughter. She couldn't bear to have the dog reminding her of her father's childish longing and when she viciously thrust at Canela with the broom, she was trying to drive away the uncomfortable memory of her unkindness.

At last the ginger-and-white dog understood that she would see the old man no more and then she did not return. She had been lonely and defenseless before but now she was even more so because, each time she found someone new to whom to give her heart, it became more difficult to live alone. In her own way she had made the old man part of her life and she could not understand why, suddenly, he had abandoned her, why he no longer came down the stairs, why he had ceased to exist.

She was driven away in fear and bewilderment and she looked into the face of every old man with such an expression that some, more observant, or more kindly, would notice and wonder for a moment. Among these, one might snap his fingers or call to her, but she slunk away as soon as she knew it wasn't the one she looked for, and they forgot her just as soon as she forgot them.

14

A Change of Luck

1

There was a five-story block of flats with a fir tree in a small garden in front of them and an open, tree-lined space to one side where the boys usually played football and baseball and tested their model airplanes. Sometimes they would shoot at the sparrows in the trees with air guns but, happily for the birds, their aim was anything but accurate.

In front of the flats, on the other side of a road, two twelve-story blocks of flats were being built. A high wire fencing had been erected about the site, to keep children from coming to harm and adults from stealing the materials, and this place was guarded at night by a guard who had two dogs for company. One was a big, brindled wolf dog, the other a mongrel of sporting breed, chestnut in color and with yellow eyes like a goat's.

Neither of these dogs actually belonged to anyone. They had spent their several years wandering from building site to building site and had doubtless been born in a similar place. They followed this workman and that but wore no collars and had no one actually responsible for them. The workmen tossed them bits to eat from their lunches but their main sustenance, since they had moved to this particular building site, came from the people who lived in the flats opposite who had got into the habit of leaving parcels of scraps by the wire fencing.

The wolf dog, who was the cleverer of the two, soon discovered where these packets of food came from and, after a while, he was barking beneath the windows, expecting things to be thrown down to him, which they were. A woman on the third floor was his particular favorite. She got into the habit of asking for scraps for him at the butcher's, and chopped up the piles of chicken claws that nobody wanted when their chickens were cleaned. He was a friendly animal, conscious of his strength, and liked nothing better than having his ears fondled and his back scratched. He had at least three names, Hambrón, Lobo and Campañilla—The Hungry One, Wolf and Tinkerbell—while his mate, the one with the goat's eyes, was typically called Linda, Pretty One, although she was anything but pretty.

Linda had seven or eight puppies twice a year, fathered by the wolf dog and nursed among the bricks and cement. She never begged or barked for food as did her mate but just waited for it to be given to her, not even protesting when the other stole it from under her nose. She was often very thin but always serene.

During the daytime, when the building site was a bustle of comings and goings, with clouds of dust and lorries dumping things noisily, both dogs preferred to laze in the shadow of the trees in front of the flats. When it was wet or cold they curled up in the doorway, which was a fairly sheltered place. Both of them would sometimes try to follow the woman who fed them up the stairs, because on a couple of occasions she had let them into her flat during the coldest days of winter. The wolf dog would thrust his nose into her shopping bag when he met her on her way back from the shops and it was a struggle to keep him from stealing the things that were there.

The children who lived in the flats were used to both dogs and weren't afraid of them. They would sometimes stroke them and give them bits of their rolls or potato crisps, but no one had any particular fondness for them except the woman on the third floor, who would have liked to keep the wolf dog for herself. She already had a dog, a fat little mongrel with huge cocked ears and tiny, piglike eyes, and there really wasn't room in her small flat for such a massive, energetic creature as Campañilla.

Another family came to live in the block of

flats, two floors above her. They also had a dog, a miniature dachshund, red brindle in color, who immediately decided that now that he was there the wolf dog shouldn't really be allowed to lie in the doorway. At first he satisfied himself with bristling up each time he saw him, then he would make sharp, snapping sallies. The wolf dog would obligingly move, as if recognizing the dachshund's right to eject him, although he was a newcomer. The dachshund lived inside the house and he didn't.

This new family, which was also very fond of dogs, comprised three daughters, Susana, Diana and Lydia, as well as the dachshund and parents. Susana and Diana were only too anxious to help feed the dogs in the doorway—Lydia was only four and was more interested in her dolls—but in fact they had plenty to eat, one way and another, and the dachshund was very jealous of any scraps that weren't put aside for him. His name was William and one of his reasons for taking such a dislike to the wolf dog was that he had seen his young mistress, Susana, feeding him.

It was cold and rainy although it was now the month of May. Linda once followed the two girls up the stairs and pushed herself into their flat without waiting to be invited. She was wet and muddy and their mother immediately pushed her out again, not wanting to encourage her, knowing how easy it was to get fond of a dog, even one as ugly as this. The goat's-eyed creature went without any protest. She hadn't expected to be received.

One morning, when the children were at school and their mother had set out to do the shopping on a gray, damp day, she saw another dog lying in the middle of the open space where the boys always played. Her long hair was dirty, her frame was exaggeratedly gaunt, and there was a look of uncaring despair about her that caught the woman's attention. She remembered the parcel of lentils that the children had forgotten to take down to the dogs and decided to go back for it for this stranger, who certainly seemed to be in need of something.

But when she tried to draw closer, the parcel open in her hands, the dog jumped up with a snarl and slunk hurriedly away, fearful distrust expressed in her amber eyes. She lay down again some way off and the woman left the open packet of food where she could see it.

"You'll come and get it if you're hungry," she said, but just then the wolf dog came up and stole the lot in spite of the woman's efforts to chase him away.

Later that day, at lunchtime, ten-year-old Susana said, "Mama, there's a new dog downstairs. Have you seen her? She's so dirty that at first I thought she was a lump of mud. But she's very pretty. Do you think I can take her something to eat?"

There was chicken and rice that day for lunch and as soon as the table was cleared, both girls rushed down with the leftovers for this new dog. She had moved back to the boys' playground but immediately slunk away again when the girls came up. Susana and Diana went back disappointed, the packet of food still in their hands.

"She wouldn't come for it and we didn't want to leave it there in case the other dog got it, greedy thing that he is."

"You'll just have to be patient then," their mother advised. "If she's hungry, she'll eat. She's obviously afraid. Someone must have ill-treated her. Leave her the food and go away."

"Suppose she's not here tomorrow? Then what shall we do?" Dark-eyed Susana, impulsive, impetuous, didn't want her to go. She wanted some guarantee that the pitiful newcomer would stay.

"What can we do?" her mother tried to console her. "If she wants to go, she'll go. If she wants to stay, she'll stay. You just leave her the food. At least she'll know we don't mean her any harm."

The next day the dog was still there. The girls took her food again, left it where she could see it and went away. They did this day after day but she would never come near them no matter how often they called to her and snapped their fingers. They tried to take her the food when the other dogs were not about, to make sure that she would be the eventual devourer of it, and their only

satisfaction was in watching her from a distance
—the timorous approach when she was sure
there was no danger, when at last she would put
down her head to sniff at the contents of the
paper. The slightest untoward sound or movement would make her jump and rush away, even
the whispering of the wind through the newspaper.

Their only consolation in all this time was
that she didn't go away. She was still there, day
after day, always out of reach, unapproachable,
and the girls were determined to gain her trust,
especially Susana.

Heeding her mother's advice, she would gradually draw closer while the dog was eating, talking
gently to her, hardly daring to breathe once she
was reasonably close. This required great effort
on her part for, normally, she could hardly keep
still for a second. Many times the dog would start
and skulk away but, bit by bit, she allowed the
girl to come closer. The snarl, which was really
no more than an empty threat, each day became
more uncertain, but she was as elusive as a sparrow.

In this way three whole weeks went by and
Susana almost despaired of ever getting close
enough to stroke her. She had already given her
a name, Shadow, which seemed to suit her very
well, so thin and wraithlike was she, so difficult
to touch, and she repeated this name over and
over again, caressingly, coaxingly, while the dog

warily gulped down the scraps that were put for her.

Sometimes Susana's mother would go down and try to talk to her and the little dachshund would sniff around her persistently. She even ran away from him.

But one day, when it was almost June and because of the constant rain the dog still looked more like a walking bundle of mud than a live creature, Susana returned home rejoicing. At long last Shadow had allowed herself to be touched. At long last her fingers had felt the dry, mud-flecked skull, momentarily it was true, but physical contact had actually been made. It was a very special day.

2

The ginger-and-white dog had no way of knowing that at last her luck had changed and that once more fortune had decided to be kind to her. A recent, cruel experience with humans had left a deep impression upon her that no memory of previous small kindnesses could erase. She had flopped herself down beside the block of flats at the end of her tether, exhausted by hunger and ever-constant fear, when the threat of death itself would hardly have moved her. By the time she was feeling better, she already recognized the fact that here was food in abundance and, as far as she could make out, no threat to her existence, so she hung around, resting, gathering strength, ineffectually snarling from time to time, but gradually regaining just a little of her utterly destroyed self-confidence.

The wolf dog made friendly overtures toward her, whereas the goat's-eyed dog took no notice of her at all. Neither offered her any threats and soon she tagged along behind them, wherever they happened to be. She let the wolf dog steal her food. She let the goat's-eyed dog steal it too. Only if there was any left when they had finished would she hesitantly approach. Luckily, there was always someone leaving scraps here and there so that in reality there was enough for all three, Shadow getting what was left when the others had helped themselves to the choicest pickings.

She discovered that at nighttime the two dogs moved back to the building site and after a while she followed them, shrinking away from the overtures of the nightwatchman, who didn't mind an extra dog on the site, lying at a distance from the fire he would make with the scraps of wood lying about. The crackling blaze attracted her. Although she no longer actively remembered the gypsy boy, she instinctively associated the flames with a sense of comfort and well-being.

For a long time she passively let the days go by, eating, sleeping, following the other dogs from place to place, running whenever a human being too closely approached. The weather improved and she even felt animated enough to pull the bits of dried mud out of her coat and from between her paws. She spent a number of hours grooming herself in the sun and, although she could never be anything but shaggily unkempt, the regular feeding and placid existence began to show itself in her improved appearance.

She saw how the wolf dog went crazy with pleasure whenever the woman from the third floor came downstairs, acting like a puppy, kicking his legs in the air, wriggling in a most undignified fashion, exposing his belly in friendship and trust. She saw how Linda allowed the children to cling around her neck, how she stretched herself out in the sun on the pathway and wouldn't even move when someone wanted to walk by, completely fearless, certain that no one would want to hurt her. She watched the workmen throw scraps to the waiting dogs, and even wrestle with Lobo in a friendly way, and when the wolf dog and his mate followed them to a nearby bar, tails wagging, she took to following also.

Like them, she grew to expect the daily packets of scraps; she grew to accept the workmen's rough voices but friendly hands; she began to forget her terrible fear and to look forward again to the arrival of a human being who meant her no harm.

In all her life she had never had so many people to care about her. Mere chance had brought her to a place where there were three dog owners and she got to know the three dogs, William, Rubi and Pinky, and their owners, equally well, greeting them all with a peculiar expression she had developed, half snarl, half grin—as if not sure whether to desert the warning in favor of the salutation. The happier she was, the more diabolical her expression became as all her teeth came into view, her body wriggled and her tail wagged furiously as she snorted and grinned in a most disconcerting way.

By midsummer she was confident enough to lie in the sun with Linda, letting people walk around or step over her without moving. At nighttime she would join her voice to that of the other two dogs whenever anyone walked past the building site, barking madly and enjoying the noise she made, for the first time in her life fearlessly daring to challenge the passing of a human being and not receiving punishment for it.

Between the workmen and the nightwatchman, the women and the children, Pinky's master, who was a retired army officer, and the two placid dogs, most of her self-confidence was restored. Hunger was a thing of the past. She chased rats and cats with the wolf dog and his mate, she slept near the nightwatchman's fire, and in the daytime she watched the children and learned not to be afraid of them.

But once again her gentle heart made her look for someone to love. The choice was varied. She had found many friends, many people she could almost trust, and she took to following them in turn, eyes hopeful, expressive searching for the one who would satisfy the never-quenched hunger of her heart.

She couldn't work things out in a human way. She couldn't decide who cared most about her by the food that was left or the children who called to her because, at one time or another, everyone gave her food and everyone caressed her. Perhaps it was because of the dogs, the dachshund, the little roly-poly mongrel, and the white-whiskered Pinky who lived in the ground-floor flat next door to the others, that she was drawn more to these three families than any other. She would follow all three of them in turn and greet all three with equal fervor, unconsciously searching for someone to accept her affection.

15

The Law Is the Law

1

By August, Shadow had another litter
of puppies to care for. She had most cautiously
sought a hiding place for them, at length giving
birth to them in the airshaft of the foundations
in one of the blocks of flats in construction. No
one knew they were there—at least, that is what
she believed—and she stayed in the dust and
darkness with them for three whole days.

At the end of this time she just had to leave
them for a while. Once she was out again in the
fresh air, stretching her legs, rubbing noses with
other dogs, hearing the greetings of the workmen
who had noticed her, and saw from her gaunt and
dirty state what she had been up to, she suddenly
felt wildly joyful. She dashed from one person
to another, allowing herself to be caressed by all
and sundry, acting like a puppy, that terrible
grin all over, gamboling, cavorting, an odd mix-

ture of happiness and instinctive fear, of tension bursting out ridiculously.

When she calmed down, she crossed the road, hoping to find something to eat, little knowing that anxious eyes had been watching out for her all these three days. The wolf dog and Linda came with her. It was early morning and they were hungry too. Lobo began to bark. Linda just sat on her haunches, looking up at the third-floor kitchen window. Shadow watched them both, tail slowly wagging, jaws apart.

Someone came down the stairs. It was the woman with the dachshund. She had some food in her hands, which the wolf dog immediately snatched. He crossed the road with the packet, intending to eat it alone, and Linda trotted after him. Shadow looked at the woman expectantly. She opened the door for her and said, "Come on, then. Come upstairs."

Shadow understood what was meant but she had never been through that doorway before, although she had watched Lobo and Linda enter several times. She was terribly unsure of herself but terribly hungry too. William kept sniffing all around her, whimpering, tail wagging. In the end, she made up her mind.

She went up the four steps to the door and crossed the threshold, ready to flee at the slightest suggestion of danger, flinching as the door closed behind her. She followed the woman up the ten flights of steps to her flat, hesitated before actually going inside, tail between her legs, almost scurrying, but slightly animated by the presence of the three girls who exclaimed with pleasure at the unexpected sight of her.

She followed them to the kitchen, three pairs of hands all over her, and watched while their mother piled up a plate with stewed meat and vegetables. When it was put on the floor in front of her she hardly dared lower her head, not really able to believe that no danger was involved. But the food was warm and appetizing and hunger suddenly overwhelmed her. She began to eat and in less than a minute the whole plateful had disappeared.

"Do you want some more?" the woman said. Everyone was watching, faces all smiles, eyes shining with pleasure.

A second plateful disappeared as rapidly as the first. William whined and rushed around her, overwhelmed by the presence of this big dog in his domain, pleased to have her but not liking the idea of her making herself so much at home. He endured while she gulped down yet a third plateful and, by this time, the cooking pot was empty and Shadow was full.

She lapped up all William's water, then went to the kitchen door, which had been shut, wanting to get back to her younglings. She fled down the stairs, as if no longer believing that no harm would come to her, and pelted across the road, forgetting caution and nearly getting hit by a car, and all because a workman was unwittingly disconnecting some pipes near the airshaft where her puppies were hidden.

After this, Shadow went upstairs to William's house nearly every day to eat and drink her fill before going back to her puppies. She only stayed long enough to clean the plates before running down the stairs again, still not able to place complete trust in the humans, still afraid that some harm might come to her if she stayed.

The workmen found the puppies in the airshaft and pulled them out because they were going to cover it with an iron grid. They put some old rags under a balcony by the doorway and placed the five furry creatures there. They all looked exactly like their sire, the wolf dog, and promised to be equally big and handsome.

One of the puppies was taken off by the electrician, although it was hardly more than a week old, and a second disappeared a few days later in a similar fashion. There were still three of them, chubby, buff and gray colored, and Shadow's greatest pleasure in spite of her nervousness was when the woman and her three daughters came to see them.

A few days later a third puppy disappeared. She couldn't know that the woman herself had taken it, having found it a home with a young married couple who wanted a dog.

By now, the remaining puppies were five weeks old and she was no longer so enthusiastic about them. She had little milk by this time and they were constantly hungry for they were big, strong and energetic. She only fed them once a day, which wasn't enough to satisfy them, and hardly went near them for the rest of the time, anxious to escape their voracious demands. The workmen gave them a dish of water, which helped, but they really needed solid food, suitable for their tiny teeth, and of this there was none at all.

Eventually the woman found homes for both of them.

2

The months went by, September, October, November, December, and wherever the woman went Shadow followed her. She followed Susana to school at nine o'clock and was back outside the flats to follow her mother and little Lydia to the nursery school at half past nine. William usually accompanied them on this trip, which was a mile-long walk beneath the trees, and he and Shadow frolicked along together, for at least she was learning to play, something she had never done since her earliest puppyhood.

Her way of playing consisted of lying in wait for William some twenty yards ahead and, although her intentions were of the friendliest, her sudden attacks were pretty devastating for his small frame. He would reach home covered with mud if the ground were damp and full of dust if it were dry. Luckily, he was solid. Then Shadow would usually follow them upstairs and have a plateful of milk and biscuits, or cereal, in the kitchen. William had to be given a small plateful, too, to keep him from complaining.

She would then go off downstairs again and wait about until Diana came downstairs at eleven to go off to her school, which was just as far as Lydia's. Shadow followed her too, and the whole story was repeated in the afternoon at half past three and half past four.

She followed the whole family everywhere, whether to the shops, the schools, the bus stop, the doctor, the cinema, wherever any of them happened to be going. After a while her dogged persistence became rather a nuisance. There was no way of preventing her determined tailing and it came to the point where the people would sometimes have to try to hide from her, or creep out of the front door when she wasn't looking.

Once she followed the woman to a friend's house and waited four entire hours for her until she reappeared. She would sit at the bus stop, watching the bus bearing the family away, a picture of dejection, and cause havoc in the doctor's waiting room, usually full of small children terrified of dogs, every time she tried to get through the door.

It was obvious to everyone that Shadow was determined to become a member of the family

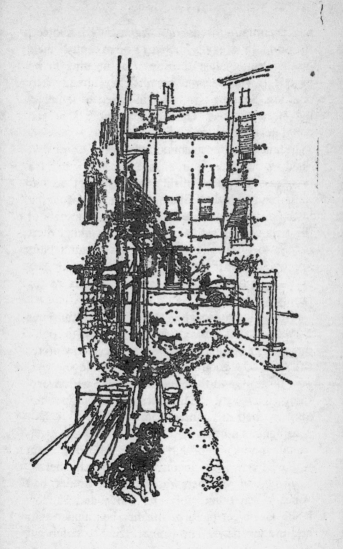

and eventually discussions began on the subject, the children begging for her to be accepted, their mother not against the idea but needing to be practical. The flat was small. They already had one dog. Shadow was, after all, used to living in the street. It was eminently possible that she could never learn to live indoors.

Meanwhile, her husband didn't even know that Shadow came up four or five times a week for breakfast. He didn't dislike dogs, in fact he was quite fond of little William, but the idea of taking in the dirty, long-haired mongrel that hung about the flats was so ridiculous that he wouldn't even bother to discuss it. He certainly wouldn't have approved of her frequent visits to the kitchen and was quite unmoved by her devotion to his family.

The children broached the subject several times a week, never losing an opportunity to point out to their mother how sweet she was, how pretty she was, how good she was, how gentle she was, how faithful, and their mother agreed with everything they said but went on answering no. Shadow had to content herself with this half acceptance and they had to put up with the occasional annoyance of having her following them where it was very inconvenient to take her.

The good weather was fading. Summer had gone. It was often rainy and windy and Shadow made an abject picture with her bedraggled hair and muddy paws. The woman tried to comb her and bought a metal comb especially for the purpose, for William's little brush was no good for her tough tangles. But Shadow showed such terrible fear of being touched and even went so far as to snap that she decided not to bother. After all, once she was down in the street again, how long would a good grooming last her?

Everybody got used to seeing the ginger-and-white dog tagging along behind the woman and the dachshund. Some people would ask if she belonged to them. The teacher at the infant school where Lydia went let Shadow come into the classroom, telling the children not to be frightened, recounting what she knew of her history and her devotion to a particular family, until some of them actually dared to touch her.

William, meanwhile, was torn between pride and jealousy. He had already convinced himself that Shadow belonged to him. The fact that she was some three times his size made no difference. He was the male and therefore the dominant figure in their relationship. He was small in size but great in dignity and when she tossed him about too much he would retaliate with extremely bad temper, his lips drawn into a savage, foxlike snarl as he flew at her with every intention of biting. This usually brought her back into line and she would leave him alone.

William discovered that if he kept close to the wall as they went along she was unable to knock him over, so he would trot along happily, tail perkily high, and as soon as the walls gave out, dash for shelter under a wooden bench or try to keep between his mistress's feet.

He got used to her coming up for a meal, although he whined and tried to steal the food from her plate. A gruff bark from her would quickly make him draw back. He was in a constant state of anxiety just as long as she was in the house, but sat by the door and whimpered miserably as soon as she had gone.

In wintertime a carpet was laid on the living room floor and Shadow quickly discovered how warm it was. But she wasn't allowed to stay on it. She had too many fleas. It was really the fleas' fault that Shadow was never allowed to stay for more than ten or fifteen minutes in the flat. The woman could visualize them being left behind when she had gone. She allowed her to stay in the kitchen because its floor was tiled and frequently washed, but in spite of everyone's fondness for her, it was impossible to overlook the fact that she was filthy and flea ridden.

The two twelve-story blocks of flats where Shadow had brought forth her younglings in the summertime were nearly finished by February. The big wire fence was pulled down, the huts where the workmen kept their tools and where the guard slept at night were knocked to pieces. Rats fled in every direction and the dogs had a fine time catching and killing them, although the wolf dog sustained several deep wounds.

The dogs were at a loss because only a few workmen remained, painters and electricians doing the last odd jobs. Children were now able to run about all over what had, until recently, been their private territory, to guard at night and from which they had savagely barked to keep everyone at bay.

Susana and Diana asked again and again, "What's going to happen to Shadow, now that the workmen are going?"

"I expect she'll go with them to another building site."

Again the question, "Can't we keep her?" and again the answer, always the same.

All three dogs more or less lived on the pavement in front of the occupied flats, completely bewildered by the sudden change in their way of life. The wolf dog and Linda had lived on the site for nearly two years.

Furniture vans began to arrive, discharging settees and bedroom suites. The dogs no longer belonged there at all. Shadow took to sleeping under a bush that hedged the pavement. The wolf dog calmly took refuge in the doorway, moving away only when he saw William come charging down the stairs to snap at him, and goat's-eyed Linda stretched herself out in the middle of the pavement as usual, completely indifferent to all that occurred around about.

No one ever discovered who it was that called the municipal dogcatchers. It was impossible to believe that anyone in those three blocks of flats, where the dogs had been fed for almost two years, would betray them thus. Perhaps someone newly arrived in the recently finished flats had called them. However it was, one morning in March, when Susana was in bed recovering from an attack of flu, a most piteous and terrified yelping broke out. A quick glance through the window was all she needed. She rushed to the kitchen, where her mother was doing some washing.

"Mama! Mama! Someone's grabbed Shadow."

Her mother dashed to the window and saw that it was true. There was Shadow cringing on the ground being dragged along by a man in blue overalls.

She fled down the stars, determined to rescue her, not realizing till she got there that the man was the municipal dogcatcher. His big gray van was parked on the opposite side of the road.

Linda was also in the grasp of another man but the wolf dog, who knew most of life's tricks and had had dealings with the dogcatchers before, had hidden himself in the neighboring doorway, where Pinky's owner took pity on him and concealed him in his flat until the dogcatchers had gone away.

The woman argued in vain for Shadow to be released. Was it her dog? No, not really, but she fed it every day. Did she have a license for it? No, she didn't. Was it vaccinated against rabies as the law demanded? No, it wasn't.

By this time, half the neighbors were looking over their balconies. Shadow was watching the woman with terrified eyes, still cringing to the ground but her panic somewhat assuaged. Linda just sat there, her yellow goat's eyes expressionless as usual.

"You can see she's well fed. You can see she's healthy. Please don't take her away. Everyone looks after her. She's not dangerous. She's never hurt anyone. She plays with the children."

The man was adamant. The law was the law, and he was only carrying out his job.

"What will happen to her then?"

"She'll be kept for three days in the pound and after that, if no one claims her, she'll be destroyed. If you want her you'll have to come for her within three days, take out a license and have her vaccinated," and he told her where the pound was, fourteen miles from the city.

Both Shadow and Linda were dragged away. Linda didn't need much dragging. She had been resigned to her fate ever since birth, but Shadow looked back at the woman with bloodshot eyes, fighting every inch, vainly digging her claws into the pavement, uttering choking yelps, and the woman just stood and watched, blinking the tears from her eyes.

Slowly she climbed the stairs. Susana had watched everything from the window of her room, had seen Shadow forcibly pushed into a tiny cage and Linda picked up by her hind legs and flung into the back of the van. Tears were pouring down her cheeks.

"Why didn't you save her?" she cried. "Why didn't you tell the man about her?"

"I did, but it was no use," and her mother explained what had happened.

"You've got to save her," insisted Susana. "We can't just leave her to die."

"We'll see what your father says," was all her mother could promise, but when he came home and the children rushed to tell him the terrible news, his only reply was, "It's about time those dogs were cleared from the street." But he laughed to hear how the wolf dog had managed to escape.

16

Welcome Home

1

It seemed that fate had dealt the ginger-and-white dog an irretrievable blow. It had taken her almost a year to regain confidence in herself, to forget her terrible fear and to find someone else to love and, more important still, have someone to care about her in return. She knew that the family did care about her, more than any of the other people who brought her scraps of food and caressed her from time to time.

At the end of the journey, she was dragged out of the little cage and pushed into a fairly large pen, which she didn't even bother to explore. She just cowered in one corner, shaking with fear and foreboding, and when the iron door was slammed shut its noise seemed to slam right through her, too.

Linda was in the cell next to her own but she

was unaware of this. She was unaware of anything but her crushing terror.

Time went by. Now and then she heard footsteps and there were dogs barking, whimpering or yelping not far away. She heard human voices, too, but they were all unknown to her and caused her to shake uncontrollably.

After a while she came out of the corner that she had immediately taken for her refuge and tentatively began to sniff about. She discovered an open hatch, which promised to lead to freedom with its smell of fresh air.

In a flash, she slipped through it, only to find that the hatch led to a small outdoor yard, whose walls were too high for her to see over and with bars all around to prevent her jumping them. The cement floor was wet and smelled of disinfectant. Miserably, she went back to her original corner, which was on wooden slats, and curled herself up. She rested her chin on a paw and sighed deeply. Her fear had gone, but despair was overwhelming.

When it grew dark she wandered outside again, sniffing around the edges of the small concrete yard. Only the vague scent of previous inhabitants clung to the walls. The disinfectant killed most odors, leaving only its own rank smell, which made her wrinkle her nose in distaste. There was a bowl of water in one corner at which she lapped, and a dish of rice and horsemeat that she ignored.

She became aware of the inhabitants of the row of cells, but not because she could see them. The smell of them was in the air and it was a smell that frightened her. It was a smell of fear, of distress. It was the smell of her own despair and she slunk back to her sleeping place, once again overcome.

There was a small, single-bar electric radiator up on the wall that was switched on at night to keep the dogs from freezing. Its frail heat was the only comfort she was to know. The night was long and filled with howls. There was wailing and barking until dawn and, although she flicked her ears and listened with her eyes open, she didn't lift her head from her paws.

The new day began, clangings and bangings, the to-and-fro of feet, voices, occasional yelps and whines. A sparrow flew down on her water bowl to quench its thirst. She watched it with pricked ears, a light coming to her eyes for half a second, then the sparrow flew away and she was alone.

Meanwhile, everyone in the two blocks of flats was talking about the dogs that had gone, and the wolf dog was stalking about on his own, lonely without his mates. Everyone agreed that it was a shame and speculated as to who could have given the word to the dogcatchers. The people who missed Shadow most were the three girls and their mother, who just couldn't get used to the idea of not having her waiting for them downstairs, with her half grin, half snarl that made her look like Dracula, and her contortions of delight that were irresistible.

They had got into the habit of looking over the balcony for her every morning, often still in their pajamas, to call out the first hello of the day, to which she would answer with wagging tail. They looked out of the balcony from habit but only the wolf dog was there, somewhat forlorn.

Someone said that dogs were very badly treated at the pound, when they weren't sent off to laboratories for vivisection. Someone else said that they were fed to the lions at the zoo. This latter did not seem very credible, but the former assertion might be true. The laboratories had to get their dogs from somewhere and what better material was there than the unwanted, unclaimed mongrels from the street?

One thing at least was certain. After three days, whether she went into the gas chamber or was converted into a scientific experiment, Shadow would cease to exist. Oddly enough, hardly anybody mentioned the goat's-eyed dog that had been dragged off at the same time. Only Shadow of the gentle eyes and timid ways was remembered.

Everyone made excuses for not going to save her. The woman on the third floor already had a dog and, besides, if her husband did let her have another one she would prefer to take in Campañilla, the wolf dog. The people on the ground floor next door had their old dog, also. Two women protested that, although they would have loved to have her, they couldn't possibly think of it while their smallest children were still in the toddler stage. It was one thing to leave scraps but something else again when it came to accepting responsibility.

"Why don't you go and get her?" Susana demanded of her mother.

"I'd like to, but how can I? She's too far away to start with."

Dogs were not allowed in public vehicles, so that it would mean hiring a taxi for the fourteen miles—there and back—quite apart from the fact that she knew her husband wouldn't allow the dog in the flat. It didn't occur to her to ask him to go in his car to get her, certain he would refuse. He still didn't know that Shadow had frequently breakfasted in the kitchen.

If only she could be sure that Shadow would be put to sleep, then somehow or another she could get her out of her mind. But supposing she were sent to a laboratory? She didn't really believe that she would ever be served up as lion meat but the thought of her being clinically tortured and destroyed was unbearably haunting.

A pall fell over the whole family. It seemed that everyone was silently counting off the hours that were left to her. No one mentioned Shadow again until, on Sunday night, before she went to bed, Susana reminded her mother, "Tomorrow is Shadow's last day."

"Stop thinking about her. We can't keep her and that's that. Tomorrow she'll be put to sleep and all her troubles will be over. She'll never be hungry or cold again and she won't keep having puppies that will have to go cold and hungry in their turn."

They had worked it out that in just over twelve months Shadow and Linda between them had produced twenty-two puppies. Of the twenty-two, only three had found certain homes. What had become of the rest?

The woman couldn't sleep that night and her husband was quite incredulous when he discovered that she was suffering so much for the dog. In the end he said, "Well, if she means as much as all that to you, I suppose I shall have to go and get her out of the pound. But what are we going to do with her, once we've got her? We can't possibly keep her here."

"I'll find someone who wants her. I'm sure I shall," she promised. "Lydia's teacher is very fond of her and said only the other day that she's thinking of getting a dog for her children. If not, the baker might know someone. He sees lots of people. But we'd better go early, if we're going, just in case. I don't know if they have a special hour for killing them."

2

The children couldn't believe their ears when the news was given out at breakfast time. Shadow was going to be saved! Shadow was going to be saved! They danced around and around and hardly knew what they were doing.

"We can't go to school!" cried Susana. "We shan't be able to think of a thing. Let us stay at home till you come back with her."

Diana seconded her opinion and little Lydia was quick to point out that, if her elder sisters weren't going to school, she couldn't go either.

They stayed at home while their parents went for the dog. It was only fourteen miles to the pound on the right road, but they took the wrong one and had to make a detour which ate up thirty-five kilometers, as well as half the morning. The woman was on tenterhooks the whole time. Supposing they arrived too late. Did the three days count from the moment they collected the dog in the street, which had been Friday at ten o'clock, or would she be given a few hours' grace?

It was midday when they reached the pound at the end of a lane full of potholes. The car jerked along in fits and starts. It looked like a prison with its high, wooden doors, all shut up. When they rang a bell a man came and asked what they wanted.

They were conducted around the pens, of

which there were some fifty in all, each one to contain a single dog, most of them occupied. Many of the dogs were of hunting breeds, pointers and retrievers. Their presence in such a place was witness to the shabby treatment their hunting masters gave them, using them in season and abandoning them to their fate when hunting was over or if they had proved themselves poor followers of game.

One pen was occupied by a litter of puppies, quarreling over a plateful of bread and milk. There were big dogs and small ones, and they looked up at the humans who halted momentarily by their cells with pathetically lost expressions. There was a world of misery in those speechless eyes.

"Is it this one?" said the attendant, pointing to a woolly brown dog. A shake of the head. "How about this one then? This one was brought in three days ago." It wasn't that one, either. "This one, then?" No. "There's another one in the next block that might be yours."

He took them along the inner corridor of the next block whose barred doors exaggerated their sense of being in a prison. He rushed past several doors but the woman halted at each, staring through the small window, afraid that Shadow might be overlooked. Sometimes a dog stared back at her. Sometimes the cell was empty.

"Are you sure she was brought here?" the

attendant asked. "I can't rightly remember her. Of course, there're so many coming and going."

"Oh yes. It was definitely here. She was brought here on Friday."

"Well, there's one more block left. We'll have a look but if she's not there. . . ."

Out into the cold gray light for an instant, then back into the next block of cells. They were mostly unoccupied. Suddenly the woman found herself looking into Linda's yellow eyes and, at the same moment as she let out an exclamation, her husband, who was peering into the cell next door, said, "Isn't this her? It looks like her to me."

The attendant shot back the bolt. Shadow flung herself at the woman with a cry in her throat that almost brought tears to her eyes. Oh, what a greeting! What joy, what disbelief, what incredible relief and happiness was expressed in every leap and whimper and contortion of that animal body. It seemed as though her heart would burst.

The children's father said, "Well, at least she's grateful. I'll say that for her," and he was obviously impressed.

Even the attendant was moved, then he said, "There're a few formalities to be seen to before you're allowed to keep her. Would you mind coming with me? I'll just chain her, as dogs aren't allowed to walk about unchained inside the precincts."

But Shadow wasn't having any chain put

around her neck, which was black from its previous chaining. She cringed, she jumped, she twisted free a dozen times until the woman impatiently suggested, "Why not let me try? I'm sure she'll let me do it."

In a moment the chain was over her ears and Shadow nervously walked, or rather jumped, skipped and frisked, out of her jail. The woman caught a last fleeting glimpse of Linda, plump with the puppies she carried inside her, who had never found anyone to love her.

Shadow couldn't stop jumping up at the woman and at the man, licking, uttering short yelps from an overfull heart. The chain around her neck terrified her but as long as it was held by the woman she could bear it. She went through a few minutes of dire panic when she was put up on the vet's table, a rope around her nose, to be vaccinated, but the woman never left her side and her amber eyes never left that human face.

At last the man came out of the office with a license and a number to put on her collar, and Shadow was free. The chain was exchanged for William's lead, which was looped around her neck, and the big wooden gates were opened. Still jumping and licking and nearly knocking the woman over, she passed through them, with a legal standing now in human law giving her a right to live.

The fourteen miles home in the car were not

so frightening because the woman sat in the back with her and kept an arm around her, and when at last she jumped out of the vehicle and found herself once again in her old haunts her delight again burst out of her.

She raced around and around the pavement, circling all the bushes, and the neighbors who happened to see her all exclaimed their surprise. She went up to them all, tail wagging, tongue lolling, body wriggling. Then she saw the wolf dog and dashed up to him too.

"Well, what shall we do with her?" said the woman to her husband. "Shall we leave her down here?"

"No. I think we'd better take her upstairs. There's not much point in getting her out of the pound if we're going to leave her in the street. They might come and collect her again one day."

So Shadow, unbelieving, followed them up the stairs cringing and nervously wagging her tail, which was almost stuck to her legs.

The children had stuck a big notice across the staircase windows. WELCOME HOME, SHADOW.

They opened the front door and William came rushing out, barking as usual. His dark eyes sparkled at the sight of Shadow. His tail went stiff. The girls all put their arms around her in turn, and around their father too for being so good as to bring her home.

"But she can't stay," he insisted. "You'll have to find a home for her."

No one believed him, of course, least of all Shadow, who had flung herself down in her corner by the door, panting, quite worn out with emotion. William sniffed all around her. He couldn't really believe that from now on she would actually belong to him.

Epilogue

It would almost be possible to write another
book about what happened next; how Shadow
gradually accustomed herself to living with people; how bit by bit she crept deeper into their
hearts and they into hers; how long it took her
to learn not to snap and tremble and try to escape when the woman groomed her; how many
months went by before she no longer scurried,
tail between legs, when the broom was got out
for sweeping the floor; how she got to the stage
of liking home comforts so much that she
wouldn't even go out when it was raining and
insisted on having her paws dried when they got
wet; how, eventually, after many hopeful, expressive glances and heartfelt sighs, she got her
way and was allowed to sleep on the sofa at
night.

After a year, she still could not bear to be

held by anyone except her mistress, and went to pieces with terror any time she had to be examined for sore ears or cut paws or some such thing. She showed her love and intelligence in so many ways, but she could never entirely dominate her fear.

She was the kind of dog that exists the world over—because luckily dogs understand nothing about nationalities, and the only language they know is of love and faithfulness—but the special thing about her was the way in which she offered herself, in spite of her terrible fear, in spite of her bitter knowledge of mankind.

Epilogue

Dogs can be bought, found, exchanged, given everywhere, but the dog that gives itself, that chooses its own master or mistress, is the one that owns the human heart more than any other.

ABOUT THE AUTHOR
AND ILLUSTRATOR

HELEN GRIFFITHS lived for many years in Lausanne, Mallorca, and London; she now makes her home in Bath, England. She had her first book published when she was fifteen and has written more than a dozen books. Her other titles include *Moshie Cat*, now available in an Archway edition, and *Grip, a Dog Story*.

Just a Dog is partly true—Shadow is a real and lovable dog who belongs to Ms. Griffiths and her family.

VICTOR G. AMBRUS is a native of Budapest, Hungary. He studied at the Hungarian Academy of Fine Arts and at the Royal College of Art in London where he met his wife. In addition to illustrating books, he now works as an art teacher.

29816 MOSHIE CAT, by Helen Griffiths. Illustrated by Shirley Hughes. The true story of a Majorcan kitten's adventures and misadventures as he searches for and finds a loving home. ($1.25)

29948 BASIL OF BAKER STREET, by Eve Titus. Illustrated by Paul Galdone. The Mystery of the Missing Twins was one of the strangest and most baffling cases in the famous career of Basil— Sherlock Holmes of the mouse world. ($1.50)

29927 PERPLEXING PUZZLES AND TANTALIZING TEASERS, by Martin Gardner. Illustrated by Laszlo Kubinyi. A fascinating collection of puzzles and teasers to challenge your wits, tickle your funny bone, and give you and your friends hours of entertainment. ($1.25)

29984 DANNY DUNN, INVISIBLE BOY, by Jay Williams and Raymond Abrashkin. Illustrated by Paul Sagsoorian. Danny Dunn and his friends have fun experimenting with a new invention created by Professor Bullfinch: a machine that can make them invisible. ($1.50)

(If your bookseller does not have the titles you want, you may order them by sending the retail price, plus 50¢ for postage and handling, to: Mail Service Department, POCKET BOOKS, a Simon & Schuster Division of Gulf & Western Corporation, 1230 Avenue of the Americas, New York, N. Y. 10020. Please enclose check or money order—do not send cash.)